MARRIAGE: A DUET

MARRIAGE: A DUET

Two Novellas
ANNE TAYLOR FLEMING

NEW YORK

Copyright © 2003 Anne Taylor Fleming

Library of Congress Cataloging-in-Publication Data

Fleming, Anne Taylor.
    [Married woman]
    Marriage : a duet : two novellas / by Anne Taylor Fleming.
        p. cm.
    Contents: A married woman—A married man.
    ISBN: 0-7868-6874-0
    1. Adultery—Fiction. 2. Married people—Fiction. 3. Cancer—Patients—Fiction. I.
Fleming, Anne Taylor. Married man. II. Title: Married man. III. Title.

    PS3606.L458 M37 2003
    813'.54—dc21

                                                                          2002027479

Hyperion books are available for special promotions and premiums. For details, contact Hyperion Special Markets, 77 West 66th Street, 11th floor, New York, New York 10023-6298, or call 212-456-0100.

Book design by Lisa Stokes

FIRST EDITION

10 9 8 7 6 5 4 3 2 1

For my mother

A MARRIED WOMAN

—〰—

"IS IT DAD?" Kate said.

"No," her brother said.

"Can it wait then? I've got to get to a press conference in three."

He wanted to say, "Three what?" She'd taken to abbreviating things this way, dropping off the last word. See you in two. Call you in five. Sometimes she meant minutes, sometimes hours, sometimes days. It drove him crazy. As if she didn't have the time to finish the sentence. As if she was in too big a hurry. As if she was too important, too hip. But he needed her. She was the only one who'd understand, the only one in the whole wide world.

"It's Mom."

"What do you mean?"

"She's acting weird."

"Of course she's acting weird. Her husband's lying there in a coma and she's sitting there in that hospital room day after day watching him do nothing."

"It's not that."

"It is that."

"No, she's acting weird in a different way."

"What—like crying, breaking down, getting angry—all that stages-of-grief stuff? You read that book I sent you, didn't you?"

"Yes. No. But that's not it. She's acting weird in a different way."

"Stevie, come on. Cut to the chase. I told you, I've got to be there in . . ."

"Yeah, in three. No, make that two now . . . right?"

"OK, all right." She took a breath.

He heard her through the phone, could see her with that teeny little flat thing—the latest of the latest of the latest technology for her—pressed to her ear, tucked under her sleek chin-length bob. That's what their mom called it, but he figured Kate would snort at the term.

"Sweetheart," she said in a new tone, "can we cut the ADD shit? What's up with Mom?"

"She looks great."

"She what?"

"She looks great all of a sudden. She isn't crying or getting angry. She's sitting there calmly day after day, almost happy. But it's more than that. She looks really, I don't know, pretty."

"So. She's always been pretty."

"No, she's making herself pretty."

"What do you mean?"

"She's actually wearing some eye makeup, I think. It looks like it."

"That's overdue. That's no biggie."

"Maybe not, but she's also dyeing her hair."

"She's what? Now? God, that is weird. I was always after her to do it. I used to kid her that she and Dad looked like the Centrum twins—with their matching silver hair."

"It gets even weirder."

"How?"

"She's doing it right there at the hospital."

"What do you mean she's doing it there?"

"She's dyeing it right there in his bathroom, with him lying there all comatose. I caught her at it, you know, all that brown goop around the hairline. And that awful smell. That's why I peeked in. I got there yesterday and she wasn't there and then I smelled that weird chemical smell so I peeked into the bathroom and there she was with a towel around her shoulders and all that brown crap on her head. She didn't see me. At least I don't think so."

"Jesus. I didn't read about this in the grief book, did you?"

They laughed together.

"Maybe she's fucking the doctor. He is sort of cute."

"For God's sakes, Kate."

"Sorry. I was just kidding."

"Yeah, well it's easy for you. You're not here to see this."

"OK. I hear you. You're holding the high cards. Want me to come down?"

"If you can."

"Let me see if I can hand some stuff off. I'll try to get down this weekend, at least for a day. Shit. I've got so much work. But I'll push it around."

"Let me know your flight and I'll come get you. Burbank might be easier. LAX is out of control. 'Course it's easier to get back to UCLA from there."

"I hear you. I'll call you later. Give Mom a kiss for me. Dad, too." There was a pause. She waited for her brother. "I'm sorry, Stevie. I know it's hard. I'll get there."

Caroline Betts did see her son peek in the door but didn't let on. As he slid backward, she permitted herself a small smile. She knew exactly what his reaction would be and what he would do next. He certainly wouldn't ask her flat out what she'd been doing in there. He might drop a, "Your hair looks good," but he would never let on that he saw her doing it in the bathroom. He would figure it would make her nervous and making her nervous would certainly make him nervous. He didn't like edging into those places. He was like his mother that way. No, what he would do is call Kate, summon her if he could. Caroline could imagine their conversation. He would say something about their mother acting weird. Kate would bluster, try not to get involved, but ultimately yield. She would come, acting hurried and burdened, but her sheer presence would calm her baby brother. She'd whirl around the bed, badgering the doctors in her lawyerly fashion: Are you sure? What about this? Shouldn't he be back in ICU? Can't we try that? Steven would say, "Jesus, Kate," a lot—more under his breath than not—but her assertive hectoring would pacify him. She would be doing again what she did when they were little: running interference between him and the world so that he could let down his guard. He would resent her with complete gratitude.

And after she was done with the doctors—she'd have them all in there, every specialist whose name she'd heard; she'd page them as she would one of her aides, standing beside her father's bed working her cell phone with frantic exactitude demanding they come soon because she was only there for a couple of hours—she would beam her aggressive and loving concern on her mother. Are you OK? Are you eating? Hey, you look awful good. Am I missing something here? What's up with the hair? But even she wouldn't bring up the fact that her mother had dyed her hair in the hospital bathroom because that would rat out her brother. That she would never do. She was stymied there. She'd have to try to trick it out of her mother some other way. But Caroline was up to it. She had withstood her daughter's forceful solicitude before. Long before Kate had become a lawyer, her mother had learned to act the part of the evasive witness in a way so deft her daughter hardly noticed—or if she noticed, couldn't effectively break down. It was their dance and, in truth, Caroline took some pleasure in it the way the not naturally articulate take pleasure in bringing to heel the verbally dexterous—with feints, shadows, silence. It was a gift all its own.

You couldn't seem obvious or recalcitrant. That just elicited irritation or more dazzling verbiage raining down on your head like a ton of bricks. No, it was a skill, one Caroline Betts had practiced all her adult life, not just with her preternaturally verbal daughter—who talked before she walked, looking up one day at her parents from all fours, at something like eight months, and saying, "bottle," not "baba" or anything like that, but a clearly recognizable "bottle," causing genetic thrills to run up and down her father's spine because he recognized her, in that moment, as his true offspring, part of his Tribe of the Hyper Articulate (so did Caroline, ceding her right then; it was not lost on her that her daughter's first word was bottle, a declaration of independence from her mother's breast)—but, earlier, with the father himself, her husband, her noisy, opinionated, garrulous husband, who now lay inert and presumably silent for the duration. Looking down at him, the huge ventilator tube taped in his mouth, Caroline felt a loneliness so complete it was as if she'd been socked in the stomach. She doubled up, trying to breathe through the tummy clutch of bereavement.

But that bereavement was inflected, ever so slightly, for one moment, with a concomitant sense of relief. Barring some miracle, there would be no more noise out of this man she'd been married to for forty years. The rap, the patter, the gibes and jokes, the bombast and bon mots and bellicosity was at end (not that that bellicosity had been directed at her; only once that she could remember—and she could remember), and the realization of the completeness of that silence left her panting—she was, she heard herself, panting in inadvertent tandem with the ventilator, *ssshhhh-pft, ssshhhh-pft, ssshhhh-pft*, in-out, in-out, in-out—with grief, ever so slightly leavened by the thought: she would return in widowhood to the calm quiet of her childhood. A full circle. And she wondered if the other near-widows she'd seen sitting in the other rooms and in the halls and the cafeteria, keeping their own vigils, were experiencing the same range of feelings while everyone looking at them, everyone looking at her—family, friends, the treacly, commiserative hospital "support staff"—assumed that in the women's hearts there was just one big yowl of impending loss instead of the complexion of feelings that rattled around in there. Everyone looked at you with doe eyes telling you you were being so brave and ought to get out of the hospital more, as if you were now a patient, too, or worse, a child, when, in fact, you'd lived nearly half a century with someone and mixed in with your stunned sense of being abandoned there were flicks and flecks of a thousand other feelings, a thousand other memories that impinged on the sweet, childlike purity of that horror of abandonment. She wondered, too, at what the other incipient widows were saying, more likely whispering or even just mouthing, to their comatose husbands in the long, bright hospital nights, the sotto voce monologues taking place in all those rooms when the phalanx of daytime attendees—the physicians and family members, the do-gooders and well-wishers—had gone home, leaving the women alone on their bedside chairs or cots (a few were sleeping there as she was; she had seen their small fold-up beds coming and going) to take their parting shots, unburden themselves finally of long-held shards of resentment or long-withheld assertions of love now that there was effectively nobody left to hear them, or certainly to respond to or rebut them, a contrapuntal chorus of epithets and endearments (please don't go, don't go . . . you stupid son of a bitch how could you do that to me . . . oh baby baby baby) Caroline swore she could hear many a sleepless night under the techno-hum that was sustaining all of their dying but still tantalizingly present husbands.

"Mom, your hair looks great. When d'you do it?"
Caroline smiled at her daughter. "Thanks. Do you really like it?"
"Yeah. Who did it?"
"I did. You know, the stuff you can buy is awfully easy now."
"I guess. I wouldn't trust myself. Anyway I just don't have the time."

"Takes as much time for them to do it as you," Stevie said.

"Right. As if you know."

The little zings and arrows. Kate doing her interrogative things. The family was in order. Three-quarters in order. Caroline smiled. The kids had arrived at noon. Caroline heard them coming from the elevator, Kate in full Kate-gear, asking Steven a host of questions, out loud, and then the suddenly whispered ones—about guess who.

They swung into the room, arms entangled, Kate looking tired around the eyes but striking, as always, a little heavier than usual, tending to William's slightly soft middle. She had the same sharp, dark eyes, dark hair, and wore clothes easily. She knew what looked good on her, simple, tailored suits—even bright ones. Her casual self was only a notch down, jeans with a blazer and always a pin or a string of pearls even with a T-shirt. Never, ever sweats or jogging shoes. Caroline herself never wore those, even here in the hospital where it was the uniform of the other women, certainly the ones who were spending nights. Caroline didn't like exercise wear—except to exercise in—and, at the moment, she was in the process of conscientious upgrading. She'd been careful not to wear any of her new clothes—she'd finally bought a few good pantsuits herself and silk T-shirts—because she knew those, in combination with her dyed hair, would drive her daughter into a direct cross, some variation of, "Mom, what the hell's going on here?" Instead, she had on her pressed jeans with a button-down pink shirt.

One of the advantages of the hospital vigil was that she was simply sending everything to the laundry—taking it rather. She'd walk her dirty clothes down into a cleaners in Westwood Village and pick them up a couple of days later. There were only a few pieces at a time, not the endless volume of William's shirts. When he was in full gear, in a trial, say, he'd go through two or three a day, bringing them home wadded up in his briefcase. He sweated heavily, always had, from the day in 1953 when Caroline had met him on this very campus, thinking it unsightly at first, off-putting, the dark stains under his armpits,

everything about him dark and noisy and gesticulative, liking it
though, the sweet strong yeasty smell of him, the minute she was first
and finally close enough to him to take it in. He was very careful with
her, unrushing, figuring her, she figured, to be a virgin still, which—
at twenty-one—she was not though she knew she looked like one, that
there was something slightly withheld about her, even prissy, with her
shoulder-length brown hair and shirtwaist dresses. But she was content
to take the time he was giving her. It was languorous, aromatic—his
particular smell filling the car where they did everything but go all the
way. Not because of Caroline. There in that musky cocoon, she would
have refused him nothing. It was he who pulled back, over and over, a
teasing restraint that set her up for explosive pleasure (did he know
what he was doing all along?) when, after six months, they finally did
have sex in his messy fraternity room one hot summer night. It wasn't
what he did to her, but what he emboldened her to do to him. He was
free and easy in his flesh in a way no other man she had been with had
come close to. In fact, she had slept with two men, eager on the first
count to shed her virginity and move on into her adult life and eager
on the second to see if the sex got any better—which it didn't much.
William never asked about her history that night or any other. He
didn't care whether she was a virgin or not. This wasn't a sport to him,
but something bigger, wider, more encompassing. He rolled and
groaned and, propped up on one elbow, smiled down at her as she
kneaded the soft flesh of his belly, soft even then, though the rest of
him was firm and young. "Gotta do something about that," he said.
"No," she said, smiling back at him and then he fell, plunged into a
heavy, limb-spent sleep, carrying her down with him into a warm,
dark post-coital cave. She was done for. In one bedding, he had ruined
her for other men and she knew it. Twenty-five years later, when she
finally did sleep with another man—or tried to—the proof of her
ruination was irrefutable.

She looked at her attractive, opinionated daughter, the very image of the father whose hand she now held and forehead she now stroked, and wondered if Kate had had any moments of such unhinged lust. Her daughter and daughter's friends—the stream of them who had come through their suburban house over the years—had been more or less of a piece, focused, driven, adamant young women who talked openly and explicitly about sex, had from about the age of fifteen. But Caroline did not sense in them, not in her own daughter anyway, the shuddering, surrendering sense of sexual longing she had felt for her husband from that first night. Of course, appearances—as she well knew—could be deceptive. Who knew a sensualist lurked beneath her own shirtwaists? William knew. He knew.

She looked at their son, quietly standing beside his sister, who had managed to summon one of the doctors—none of the specialists, this being the weekend, just the young intern who had drawn weekend duty—and was interrogating him. Kate had done her homework as always, grilling him about every procedure that had been done since she was last here. Steven, looking slightly pained, drumming a few fingers on his sister's arm, moving them a little—as if to stop her and comfort her at the same time. They looked alike standing together, but it was as if someone had taken an eraser and smudged Kate's defined edges. Caroline always figured that Steven had inherited some of his father's sensuality, but not the energy to back it up. He'd had girlfriends since high school, one after the other, but there was never much voltage. At least, she thought, looking at both of her grown children looking down at their father, they might not know the kind of pain she had been knowing.

Steven caught her eye, pleadingly, and pantomimed eating. "Sweetheart," Caroline interrupted Kate, "let's let the doctor go now and get something to eat."

"Good idea," Steven said, as the young intern slipped away. "I convinced our new young chef to come in for lunch to do something special for you guys. I thought it would be . . ."

"I don't want to take the time," Kate said. "My plane's at four and I want to stay here with Wills." She'd called her father that since she was a child. Willy first, then Silly, then Wills from about six on.

"Sweetheart, I think it'll do us good to get out."

"You should talk, Mom. You never leave here. Look, eating is just not my priority right now. No offense."

"No offense. That should be on your tombstone," Steven said.

"Shit, this isn't exactly the place to be talking about tombstones. You guys go. I'm not hungry anyway."

"Honey, maybe you and I can go later in the week," Caroline said to her son. "Let's just go down to the cafeteria and grab something while Katie stays with her dad for a while. She'll join us if she feels like it."

As they left, Kate was whispering some off-color joke to her father. Mother and son heard the beginning of it, something about lesbians and government workers. It was their lifetime habit, the swapping of jokes. Kate gathered them like presents to bestow on her father in late-night calls. Caroline would hear him in the library roaring and then, because he knew his wife didn't much like jokes, quieting down to tell an equally raunchy one back to his daughter. It was a tribal rite, umbilical lingo—the more X-rated the better. Even in her most adamantly feminist twenties, Kate would still, to her father's delight, laugh at dumb blond jokes—and worse. Much worse.

"It's odd," he once said to Caroline, "in this generation, the girls got all the balls."

"Is that good or bad?" she said.

"Both," he said.

Caroline remembered this as she and Steven walked toward the elevator. It's funny how things seemed to float up unbidden— snatches of conversations, scenes. Things were floating, she was floating. Through the corridors, through the days, through the nights. It all felt so unreal and so hyper-real at the same time, as if she'd never lived anywhere else but in this hospital. She looked at her son's face.

"I just hate her sometimes," Steven said, flattening himself against the wall to let a gurney past.

"I know," she said. "But it's a tough time. We're all doing what we know to do."

"Right."

"She's acting a little bossy. That's what she does. You're eating and I'm dyeing my hair."

"Right." He laughed.

"It's all so weird," he said, tears coming.

"I know, baby." She held him 'til the elevator opened and a young girl got off with an armful of books.

"Oh great, you're here," Caroline said to her. "Go ahead to the room, but wait outside, will you, 'til my daughter's done. She's with him now. I've got my beeper so if you need me . . ."

"Sure. I know. Anything happens or anyone comes, I'll beep you."

"We'll only be gone about an hour. We're just going downstairs."

They rode down holding hands, mother and son. "Mom, what's she about? You're never out of here and anyway there's plenty of nurses that jump every time something beeps."

"I just like someone of my own there, that's all. What if . . ."

"What? He wakes up? Come on, Mom."

He turned to hold her.

By the time Kate joined them in the cafeteria, Steven was making oil and vinegar dressing, whisking it in a saucer with a fork. He'd managed to convince one of the women behind the counter to dig him up a bottle of olive oil and vinegar. He always carried his own little packets of Dijon mustard—he and Caroline had gone through dozens trying to "tart up," as Steven said, the various hot dogs, hamburgers, and salads they'd eaten down here over the previous three weeks. Mother and son liked fiddling with food. It intimated normalcy, pleasure, even here in this antiseptic dining hall—everyone and everything looking scrubbed within an inch of their lives, the disjunctive smells of disinfectant and grease hanging heavy in the air.

Katie looked deflated. She slid into the family quietly, conciliatorily. "Hey bro, let me have some of your salad, will you?"

It was a standard joke. Kate never ordered her own food. She just nibbled off everybody else's plate. Early on it seemed to be about dieting. Now it was just a habit. She didn't slow down enough to concentrate on what she wanted to eat, so she just grazed off other people's meals, a tendency that annoyed some of her colleagues and friends but—now lifelong—amused her family. William did it, too, leaving Caroline and Steven to make sure they always ordered enough to share.

"Hey, did I tell you guys Jamie's getting married?"

Steven, mouth full: "No shit. Who?"

"I don't know, but I hear she's already pregnant."

Caroline looked for a twitch of regret in her forty-one-year-old daughter, but if it was there, she didn't see it. Jamie had been her husband. After dating all through college, they'd married at the beginning of law school and divorced at the end, Kate doing the leaving. He was shattered and had spent the next Christmas huddled in the guest room of the Bettses' house. Kate was in New Orleans at a seminar, leaving her mother to bind the wounds she had inflicted. And then he was gone, for good, having been part of their lives and Kate's for seven years. This was the first anyone had mentioned him in years. He was to be a father. He might have been the father of her grandchild, Caroline thought, hers and William's. Increasingly, Caroline figured there would be none of those. Kate had settled into a succession of married men (she alluded to them from time to time) while Steven, at thirty-seven, seemed perennially young, content to cohabit casually with women who worked in the restaurants he worked in. So between them, Kate and Steven seemed childproof. William had asked her once if she minded not having grandchildren.

"I don't know," she said. "What about you?"

"I don't know either," he said. "It's weird, isn't it, to think that it's somehow the end of us."

That's what came back to her sitting here listening to Kate talk about Jamie, all of them waiting in effect for William to give them a sign to let go of him, untether him—and without talking about it, that's in effect what they were doing here, eating these lousy meals, riding up and down the elevator, grilling the doctors, that's what everybody was doing, the other little family pods that rode up and down with them, ate with them, nodded distracted hellos of recognition, they were all doing the same thing. Some of them did have kids in tow, the next generation, and there was something life-giving in their shrieks and whines, Caroline thought. But she didn't badger her own children about not having children. She didn't even bring it up. She was cool. She knew the drill. She didn't intrude.

"Why do you think they don't have them?" William said.

"I don't know exactly. A lot of their friends don't have them either. It's in the air."

"Maybe," he said. "But maybe they figured they couldn't be as happy as we were."

When would that have been? When would he have said that?

"Hey," Katie blurted, a piece of iceberg on her lower lip. "Want to hear the punch line?"

"OK."

"What do you get when you have fifty lesbians and fifty government workers in the room?" She took her dramatic pause. "A hundred people who don't do dick."

"Are you sure you should say stuff like that?"

"Shit, Steven. It's just a joke." Then, after glaring at him for a minute: "I miss my Wills," she said, beginning to sob.

"Sweetheart." Her mother reached across to put a hand on her bowed head. Steven, sitting beside her, stroked her back.

"I'm sorry about the restaurant," she said to her brother, gargling tears. "I would like to go. Maybe next weekend. I'll definitely come back. It's getting closer, right?"

She looked up at her mom, looking hopefully for a contradiction, and then eyeing her sharply said: "Jesus, Mom, you do look great. What the hell's going on?"

"What do you mean?"

"The hair, the eyeliner."

"I don't want to fall apart in here."

"Yeah, but when d'you dye it?"

"I told you. I did it a few days ago."

"Yeah I know, but where d'you do it?" catching Steven's eye as she asked, the two of them exploding into laughter.

The next day was Sunday. Caroline always loved Sunday. She stretched out on her narrow cot, trying to uncramp her legs and back, trick her body into relaxing against the vigilance it immediately assumed upon waking. She heard the reassuring *ssshhhh-pft, ssshhhh-pft* and knew William was still there. She didn't look over. She looked the other way, out the window, and saw the sun through a slat in the blind and heard a church bell and then under it, the screech of an approaching siren. No need to tense up. Their siren had come. She listened to it, the ambulance pulling, it seemed, right under their window and then the slam of doors and it was over, the hospital had taken in someone else—loved ones to follow. The church bells reasserted themselves and she drifted out toward them into those other long-ago Sundays, the ones before the kids and the pancakes and the cartoons, before they even had a TV. There were only a few years of them. The kids came fast. They both wanted them. But it was the Sundays before she now wanted, when they stayed in bed the whole day. William, in however deep a sleep, would

wake to the four A.M. thud of the newspaper and immediately have to
go get it. It was a challenge, information to be digested. They'd read as
the morning light came; he'd read to her, orating, denouncing, com-
mentating, and then, dropping the paper around him as suddenly as
he'd taken it up, refocus his passion on his new wife, and they'd rattle
and crackle around among the pages, his body arching toward her
mouth—hers, in turn, toward his—sleeping then, deep deep in their
cave, waking well into the day, newsprint on their hands and flanks.

"See," he said, pointing to a dark-stained patch on his buttocks,
"this is the 'News of the Week,' " grinning at her over his shoulder as
he disappeared into the bathroom.

So went the day. They made serial trips to the bathroom, one or
the other, and serial trips to the kitchen, bringing back bread and
cheese and cold beer—icy cold because on the last trip one or the
other had remembered to stick it in the freezer—reversing the normal
order of things and having scrambled eggs for dinner. They'd eat and
read and talk and pee, then again be mutually and lustfully captivated
and then fall asleep. She'd fall asleep, head on his belly, his soft penis
in her mouth. He'd fall asleep, lips still around a nipple. They'd wake
and dream-plan out loud. He'd finish law school and practice in a
good firm doing good works. She'd go on teaching until they had
kids—one girl, one boy; do you think we should have the boy first or
the girl?—and then stay home if she wanted. He didn't care if she did
or didn't. Work, stay home. It was up to her. He wanted her happy.
He wanted to make her happy—grinning again with a little bit of a
leer—right here, right now, if that's OK with you.

There were other Sundays, later ones, pleasing in their own way.
When the kids were first old enough to pad down the hall and bounce
onto their newspaper-strewn bed. When she and Steven started to
cook together and elaborate omelettes and homemade rolls came out
of the kitchen. Later, when they were first empty nesters and working
at a foundation in the inner city—she tutoring, he giving legal advice

(what was it: '77? '78?) and they'd bring home a gaggle of noisy ten-year-olds for Sunday barbecues. Then—a few years later still—when Katie moved back in for a while right after law school and she and her father, nursing wine, fought the ritualized summer Sunday evenings to an ebullient oratorical draw.

"I hate you," she remembered Katie saying to her father one of those nights, but there was amusement in her voice. "My friends all get to hate their fathers because on some level they turn out to be pigs. You're just too damn fair," she said.

"Ain't it a bitch," he said.

They had both laughed while upstairs, overhearing through an open window—it must have been hot, they were sitting outside on the back patio—the wife and mother was smiling. Good, solid Sundays, but an intrusion now as she lay on her cot trying to remember, with exactness, the earlier ones when she, a young bride, said, on successive sabbaths those words she could hear in the nights here: baby baby baby. And then: fuck me. That was the rest of it. Baby baby baby fuck me, a singing, sighing incantation, imploration, that now, out of her cot, leaning over her husband's bed, she whispered deep into his chest—going in and out with the awful artificial regularity of the ventilator—trying to breathe his signature smell, almost denuded now through inactivity and medication, inhaling deeply. Baby baby baby fuck me, a word Caroline had never said anywhere else to anyone else, not as a sex word, not as a swear word, never anywhere but in the bedroom with him. Oh baby baby baby. Fuck me.

"Mrs. Betts."

The girl stood shyly in the door with her customary armload of books. She was whispering.

"Sorry. I didn't mean to intrude."

Caroline, looking up startled, hauled herself back into the present.

"No, no, it's OK. I overslept. It's already ten?"

The girl looked at her watch. "Ten-thirty. I'm a little late."

"Just give me a minute. I'll just tidy up and be off."

In the bathroom, Caroline splashed cold water on her face, amused for a moment to see her brown hair. She kept forgetting, between mirror bouts, that she'd actually finally done it. Not so bad, she thought, poking at the roots. Not so bad. She wondered what William would say. He always said, "You're a natural beauty. You don't need to do anything." So she didn't. A good haircut, staying in shape by walking. That she did. And a little pale lipstick. But that was about it. Her brows and lashes were dark anyway and remained so, even as her hair had grayed, so she figured, that's enough. Don't push it. But things were different now. She'd lost her audience. She pushed around in her new little makeup bag for the mascara. She didn't have the energy or steady hand for the eyeliner, but the mascara she could manage. A few strokes and a shirt change and she was ready.

"Is it hot out there?" she smiled at the girl, trying to reassure her now, not sure exactly what she had seen or heard.

"Yeah, for this time of year. But, you know, it's always like this around finals. It's like some cosmic joke."

"Finals. That's right. I always forget about the quarter system. Isn't it weird taking tests in March?"

"I guess."

The girl was done with her and vice versa. They'd done their dance of normalcy in the most abnormal of situations. Like eating with Steven. Like him making salad dressing in the cafeteria. Like Katie calling—brisk and full of work.

"You've got your beeper. I've got mine. I'll just wander down and be back in maybe an hour and a half."

"Cool." The girl already had her head in her book—some sort of math or science from Caroline's cursory glance at it.

She went down in the elevator, an elderly patient in a wheelchair and the bootied attendant the only other passengers. She registered them only on the surface, a quick snapshot. She didn't want to think about anyone else in here, their dramas. She wanted to stay wholly in her own. It was warm outside, an unseasonal wind, a hint of the Santa Anas everyone was always making such literary fuss about. She had her route, her new routine. She walked for about forty-five minutes, up and around the campus and back down into Westwood Village, carefully avoiding her own two-story, yellow clapboard house in its leafy cul de sac. It was just north of the campus, an easy target, but now to be avoided at all costs, containing, as it did, almost every single marital memory she had. Today, as on most days, the village was eerily quiet—not just because it was Sunday but because it had completely changed over the years, dried up somehow. There'd been a gang shooting one hot summer day, ten years earlier, and it had quelled the street life. That and the proliferation of suburban cineplexes, so nobody came to the quaint old village theaters. She and William did. In fact, he was stubborn about not seeing movies unless he could walk from the house. She passed his favorite now, the oldest—dirty vanilla stucco with a now highrise-dwarfed spire—where they'd necked as newlyweds, the springs palpable through the plush maroon seats even then, William reaching to place her hand on his erection. Next stop was the newsstand for the Sunday papers and then on to Starbucks to get her iced cappuccinos—two of them to see her through the day—and a final pit stop at the deli for a chicken salad sandwich on rye, hold the mayo. Her standard supplies. This was her third Sunday. She figured she might eke another after this, maybe two, and all she wanted was for this one to go as slow as possible.

Back in the room, she nibbled at her sandwich and read to William out of the papers. Everything was about Clinton and his dalliance with "that woman." William had hated it—loved it and hated it.

"Are they crazy? They're going to throw a man out of office for getting a blow job?"

He had said that, at high decibel, at their last dinner party when some of their longtime friends had been caustic about Clinton's character and appetites.

"For God's sakes guys, you don't really want to live in a country where this is going to go down—no pun intended."

There was real heat in it, as always with William, and humor. Later in their bedroom, he had tried to take it all up again with her.

"I agree, dear," she'd said, the dear coming out wrong, pacifying. It was not a word they ordinarily used, only she sometimes to do what she was trying to do now, calm him down a little.

"I'm going to call Katie," he had said. He wasn't done. He wanted more argument, more talk.

"Good idea," she had said. It was, by the illuminated bedside clock, almost 11:30, but Katie never cared. He could call anytime and she would match his energy and outrage.

"Don't wait up," he'd said, leaving the room, smiling over his shoulder (his pacifying grin). She didn't. That was a Sunday, too, as she remembered. A string of Sundays, wonderful sunny Sundays, fun days, sin days, Sundays, sinny sunny Sundays. They piled up around her as she dozed off, the newspapers slipping off her lap onto the floor.

"Mom. Hey."

Steven was gently shaking her.

"Oh sweetheart. I must have drifted off."

She noticed it was dark out. She'd slept away part of her day and wanted it back. He saw the look, the loss. He read her well, like Katie read her dad. It was as if each had been allotted a child, his child, her child.

"Are you OK? Nothing new is there?"

"No sweetheart. Nothing new. What have you got?"

"Dinner," he said, as he began unpacking his paper bags, plastic containers of food, one after the other.

She laughed. He was doing their thing, feeding them—him and her. He pried off the lids and the room filled with comforting smells, exotic ones, too.

"Our new chef is trying things so I figured we'd give him a free consult. Here, try this: crab tamales with cilantro sauce."

"Sounds awful fancy," she said, rooting into the container, then taking a forkful. "No, it's good. Maybe a little less cilantro in the sauce. What do you think?"

So it went: they swapped entrees, commenting all the while, making a ceremony against their grief. Steven occasionally glanced at his father but said nothing and Caroline said nothing either. They talked food. For dessert, there was a mango crème brûlée ("I'm not sure the mango adds anything." "Me neither.") and something called a chomeur that tasted like mashed-up bread pudding ("Baby food," Caroline said, "but good," making Steven laugh. "Yeah, a keeper," he said. "I'll tell him."). He'd even brought a Thermos of strong coffee ("Don't worry, Mom, it's decaffeinated.") and one of the little airplane bottles of brandy.

"Thought this might help you sleep," he said.

They cleaned up together, filling the bags with garbage, straightening the newspapers, and suddenly the set was struck and it looked again like what it was: a hospital room with a dying man in the middle of it. No, a hospital room with a man being kept alive in it. That's what it was and that was different. It was a different set with different requirements from the supporting cast and Caroline knew that full well. She was trying to get there. Steven knew that. In her bossy way, Katie did, too. They were just all trying to get there.

"If we can't get out next Saturday when Katie comes, will you bring the food again," she said to her son. "This is fun."

"Sure, Mom. It is fun."

He kissed her and for the first time that night turned to touch his father, brushing his lips across his forehead, then leaving quickly with his bags of trash.

Caroline washed her face but didn't brush her teeth. She didn't want the toothpaste to ruin the taste of the brandy. She turned off the light and lay down on top of the cot. She drank the brandy, willing sleep. But she'd slept so much of the afternoon that it eluded her. She finally got up and took a sleeping pill. William's doctor had given her some. She wasn't much of a pill taker so she took half and then, impulsively, swallowed the second half. She didn't want to be awake as Monday came, a new week starting, didn't want to sense tonight the other women keeping vigil in their rooms and hear again, without hearing, the murmurings of their unfinished business.

Early the next morning, the girl finally came, slipping into the room through Caroline's dreams. She was as she had been then, tall, quick-smiled, dark bangs falling into her eyes. Maybe twenty-four, twenty-five. Braless in a T-shirt and faded jeans. Makeup? Caroline strained to see through the foggy overlap of dream and memory. She moved straight to William's side, brushing past Caroline as if she wasn't there. Oh Wills, she said, using Katie's name, smiling down at him: what's happened to you? She leaned to kiss his forehead and then, straightening, started to yank the ventilator tube up out of his throat and chest. No, Caroline heard herself scream. Stop it. Stop it. But the dream was split screen, Caroline on one side, the girl and William on the other. She was frantic, but she couldn't navigate across. She couldn't get over there. The girl kept pulling at the thick tube while Caroline, distraught and sobbing, kept yelling from her side of the screen. No, No, No. She yelled for a doctor, a nurse, but nobody heard her, nobody came and the girl just went on pulling and tugging, not roughly, but adamantly. And finally she pulled the plastic tube up out of his throat. Caroline gasped. He would die now. It would be over. Her sobs had muted to weeping. She was quiet; all she could do is watch. He would die on that side of the screen without Caroline next to him, holding him. But instead of that, he smiled up at the girl, his big grinny smile, and she leaned over to kiss him on the mouth. No, no, no, Caroline said again, but this time softly. No, no, no, please no.

He was smiling. The girl was asking about Katie, how she was doing, and William, pridefully, was telling about her job in Sacramento as assistant to the speaker, how feisty she was. He even bragged a little about his son's cooking. The girl kissed him again and said: it's a beautiful day, let's go for a walk. OK, he said, let me just get out of this damn smock. They laughed. The girl had a bigger, deeper laugh than her slight frame indicated she would have. When William stood up, Caroline could see that his hair was black again and thick. He went into the bathroom and Caroline watched the girl move around the room, looking at things. She scanned the headlines in the *New York Times*, folded where Caroline had left it on the window ledge, then moved around the bed and picked up a picture of her, Caroline, with William and the kids. She looked at it without expression, then set it down. William appeared in his khakis and a white tennis shirt. Ready? Absolutely, the girl said. He held out a hand and she took it and they sauntered out of their screen into Caroline's and then right by her out the door and into the corridor and she could hear them chatting and laughing as they went toward the elevator and she tried to scream but she couldn't. Nothing came out.

Something had come out though and the night nurse, who had come to check on William, was shaking Caroline quite roughly to wake her up.

"Mrs. Betts. Mrs. Betts. Wake up. You're having a bad dream."

Caroline was vaguely aware of being touched and talked at, but resisted. The sleeping pill had her, and the downward drag of the dream was powerful. She half wanted to stay in it, because he was there, young and healthy, and half wanted to get out of it, back into whatever present there was. She gyrated in limbo, trying through the druggy fog to decide which was the path of most hope, least pain: to go back in there, into the dream, or fight back up into the present. The nurse was persistent.

"Mrs. Betts, come on now," as if calling someone out of an anesthetic. Caroline focused on her.

"Thata girl," she said, and Caroline, for all her grogginess, managed a weak smile. When did you stop being a girl? Never apparently, not to this nurse half your age, with her big burnished African-American face. 'Atta girl. Caroline closed her eyes just for a minute and saw instantly that split screen again—the dream that close to consciousness, just the next layer down—and the nurse was on her again.

"Come on now, come on." She suddenly, out of nowhere, had a glass of water and was very professionally cradling Caroline's head against her generous breast while forcing her to swallow.

"Come on. Thata girl, shake it off. Shake it off. Good. That's good. Just drink a little more."

Caroline was now inescapably awake, though the residue of the dream hung so heavy she half-expected, upon checking, to see that William's bed was empty and that he had somehow miraculously awakened and walked out of the room. But he was there, tethered to all his machines. She heard them now, their perversely comforting beeps and blips. All was in order. She was here with him and the girl was gone. The nurse turned out the overhead light and left the room.

"I'll check on you two in a little while," she said.

Lying there, Caroline said it for the first time in her life. Damn you, first. And then bolder, the ventilator doing its metronomically wheezing thing, the morning light still at least three hours away, she said out loud: fuck you. Not with much force, almost just to try it out. She almost smiled saying it. Almost. Fuck you. Fuck me. Oh baby baby baby. Fuck you.

It was Katie who had brought the girl home as a present for her father. She'd been doing that since grammar school, dragging her newest pal home to meet him, hoping they'd be mutually charmed. It was that same summer she moved back in after law school (but clearly after the night Caroline had fallen asleep smiling hearing Katie tell her father: I hate you; he saying, ain't it a bitch). Katie didn't have a job yet. She was helping in the office of one of her father's friends and that's where she met April. Both were waiting to take the bar. They'd meshed easily, not because April was as noisy and argumentative as Katie, but the reverse. She was quieter, more thoughtful, a good foil. Neither was part of a pair—Katie's divorce was just being finalized and April's boyfriend had moved to San Francisco. She was living with some other young women and they did most of their studying there, at that apartment, but her name started to float through Katie's conversation and around the Bettses' household. That's how it always went: Katie would become enamored, the name of the new enamoree would increasingly surface at the dinner table and then she would be brought home—the grand presentation. So it was this time. One Sunday, Katie finally brought April home for one of their extended-family barbecues, bringing her by the hand into the living room and, beaming, directly up to her father.

"Dad, this is April, April my father."

"I've heard a lot about you," April said.

"Not nearly so much as we've heard about you," he said, putting his arm around his daughter. "Caroline," he said loudly, looking around for his wife, "here's the famous April." The girl colored ever-so-slightly— her skin was tawny so it was hard to see, though Caroline remembered noting it as she came up with hand out, welcoming and maternal.

"Nice to meet you at last," Caroline said.

"Can I help?" the young woman said.

"No, stay with the other talkers," Caroline said. "Steven (she realized April didn't know Steven)—my son's with me. That's the division of labor around here. It's very feminist," she said, maybe a tiny bit archly and turned quickly to go back to the kitchen, because the sudden libidinal charge in the room, in that spot of the room where her handsome, just graying-at-the-temples, soft-bellied husband was smiling at this tall, tawny-skinned young woman who was smiling shyly—shyly but not so shyly—back at him, was as unmistakable as the sun coming up, or someone turning on a bright light, leaving Caroline in the shadows. Had there been a photograph taken right then it would have captured, freeze-frame, an inclination. They weren't even touching or leaning toward each other, just standing there in her living room, her tattered, well-used, wood-paneled living room—always a little dark for Caroline's taste, always meant to do something about it, maybe paint the beams white, but they'd never gotten around to it. Now there was this blinding circle of light in it. And in that circle stood her husband and a lovely, sly-shy young woman smiling at each other with such palpable mutual inclination that Caroline was amazed everyone else hadn't stopped to look. You can pray then, as you carry food from the kitchen, bringing out plates, taking plates back, smiling, chatting with old friends, you can pray that you're wrong, that you haven't seen what you think you've seen or that it's just a momentary shiver of electricity that will fizzle, go nowhere, a momentary sign of mutual appreciation, that's all. Or, in a madcap preemptive strike, you can drop all the plates on the floor and scream out: I know what's happening, or about to happen. Don't do it. Or you can do nothing and just hold your breath, no scenes, no sudden moves.

Caroline saw her only one more time. She and William met the two young women—Didn't they indeed seem young? Caroline was married and had a baby at their age—for dinner at a local Italian restaurant. They'd walked, husband and wife, hand in hand, down into the village to meet them, sharing a bottle of mediocre Chianti while they waited, William being comfortingly William, full of stories about his day, but also solicitous of Caroline's stories from her day tutoring in the "hood," remembering, with his lawyerly recall, the names of some of the kids she'd talked about, some of the ones who had been in their house for barbecues. "How's Latisha?" he asked. "How's Kevin?"

Then they came, sliding into the booth in their skirts and jackets, baby lawyers, pretty baby lawyers with pearl studs in their ears. They all shared a couple of plates of fettuccine and a pizza, the girls growing rosier and more voluble with the wine. The restaurant was chilly inside; unbidden, William took Caroline's pale blue cardigan from the back of her chair and put it around her shoulders, smiling at her as if to say: we did a good job, didn't we? These are nice girls, full of spunk and dreams. April, under prodding by Katie, talked about growing up in San Francisco, about her parents being divorced and how her father took her and her sister to North Beach for Saturday lunches and taught her to twirl her pasta with just a fork, down in the bowl, no spoon, and about the winter days when the bay was so bright and sun-splashed it hurt your eyes. They had more wine and talked about their futures, the young women did, about getting into politics, making a difference, defending women's newly won rights.

"Terrific," William beamed, "your mother and I are too . . ." He didn't finish the sentence. The waiter was suddenly there. William ordered espressos all around and that frothy stuff, you know Caroline, what is it?

"Zabaglione," she said.

"My wife," he said to April, "remembers everything."

They ate again and drank more and talked over and at each other, now, the decibel level high.

"Daddy, I almost forgot, I have a joke for you," Katie said. "Cover your ears, Mom. April, you, too. She doesn't like them either," Katie said to the table.

They smiled at each other, Caroline and April, covering their ears, uncovering them as the laughter began. "You guys," Caroline said, looking at her watch. Then to William: "Sweetheart, we need to go. I have to be on the freeway by seven."

He didn't hesitate. He asked for the check. On the street they all kissed and hugged.

"You coming home now, Katie?" her mom asked.

"We might have one last drink somewhere," her daughter said. "Don't worry. I'm . . ."

"Yeah, we know," her parents said as one: "You're a woman of the world."

They walked home, buzzy with booze in a still-pleasant way and quiet. Caroline realized the knot in her center had loosened. She'd invented the whole thing. She'd had a moment of midlife paranoia. At home, William disappeared into the liquor closet and came out with a bottle of cognac someone had given him for Christmas two years before.

"I know you have to be out of here early, but why not?" he said, waving the bottle and two small glasses as he came into the bedroom. They lay together, she propped on pillows, he beside her on his elbow, sipping the brandy.

"I'd forgotten how good this is," she said. "A person could get a taste for it."

"A person could," he said, grinning, leaning to kiss her breast through the soft nightgown.

The next day it read differently, the evening. Upon recollection, it turned itself all around. She saw the signs. They piled up as she drove down the smoggy freeway: that unfinished sentence, William about to say, your mother and I are too old, but shaving off the end before the waiter reappeared—before not after—offering dessert and coffee; April ducking his kiss, turning her head as they stood on the street saying good-bye, everybody kissing everybody but the two of them. No, they didn't dare. They didn't even flirt at dinner, Caroline now realized, because there was, underneath, some incendiary carnal excitement, what had been there in the living room, what she had walked up to and quickly walked away from. This was a girl not like Katie and her other friends, the myriad numbers who had come through the house. This one, if you listened to her and watched her, had more nerve endings, more apparent appetite. She didn't just talk politics and feminism and law—or, for that matter, dating or men. She talked about food and weather, eating pasta, the sun on the water. And she hated the bawdy jokes. William would have liked that even as he liked sharing them with his daughter. And she was his type—tall, dark-haired, slender. No big-breasted blondes for William Betts. And her laugh, bigger than expected, coming from way inside—the way essentially serious people laughed at the absurdity of things. He would like that, too. It was all there if you wanted to look at it.

Caroline never saw her again. Over the next month, April's absence from their house and from Katie's conversation became noticeable, another tip-off. One night at dinner Caroline—ever so casually—said: "Where's your friend?" not trusting herself to say the name.

"You mean April?" Katie said easily. "Her boyfriend's back in the picture. She's spending a lot of time in San Francisco."

"That's too bad," William said. "She was nice." Caroline watched him watching her though his head was down. It was all there if you wanted to look at it.

The shirts finally did it. Nothing overtly had changed. He came and went to work, called two or three times a day, made love to her with no seeming diminution or augmentation of ardor, no flares in the night, no warning signals. And yet. And yet. He was not changing shirts anymore. He came and went in the same one, even though his workload was intense, his shirts, when he came home, crumpled with the daylong dried scent of him. It wasn't that he didn't have time to change because the work was too much—it was always too much—or even that he was trying to grab spare minutes with the other woman (there it was, that's who she was, however young: the other woman). It was something else and somehow Caroline knew it, intuited it. Her rival didn't want him to change shirts, asked him playfully but seriously not to. Caroline, watching him come home day after day in the same shirt he'd left the house in, knew that with a terrible certitude, knew that the young woman liked to inhale of him the way she did, still did, deeply, face against his chest, shirted or unshirted, the way she had twenty-seven years earlier and she hated her for it, hated and envied them both, not for what they might or might not actually be doing in cars, in beds, on the office floor—the sex, the touching and kissing and nibbling, which she could not not imagine even as she tried not to—but for the beginningness of it all, the sinking-down-into-it-ness. It was her curse to remember in sharp detail standing herself on that same precipice with William—her gifted, her savory lover, her husband of twenty-seven years who was now, for the first time in their marriage, elsewhere.

She had no intention of calling his bluff, making a sudden move, if she could help herself. She would stay calm. Her behavior was part conscious, part unconscious: do nothing, draw no lines in the sand. And she was good for that for another month, until Katie went away to visit her brother who was cooking that summer in a seaside restaurant in Miami. Caroline had been relieved he was away. He would have noticed something in his mother and been commiserative in a way that would have made her crumble. Luckily he was blithely off being an apprentice chef, sending letters home full of lavish descriptions of seafood stews and crabs this or that. Caroline, all pretense of normalcy, read them out loud to William and Katie at dinnertime.

"Jesus, is that all he thinks about?" his sister said.

"Don't knock it," her father said laughing. "In the future, he'll cater our parties for free."

Oh, Caroline said to herself, so there is to be a future?

The night of the day Katie left, Caroline, unable anymore to accede to her own studied calmness, said simply, over dinner: "You're seeing her." No name, nothing else.

They were sitting across from each other at the dining-room table.

William looked up. He didn't look startled or caught off guard. There might have been, she thought, an actual flicker of relief. He didn't say anything for a long time, then: "I've never lied to you."

"You might try," she said, aiming for humor that fell flat. "Is it serious?" But it wasn't really a question because she knew the answer. Again, he didn't say anything for a long time.

"I'm a serious man," he finally said.

"Then how," she said, "can you sleep with someone named after a month?" He managed a pained smile.

"Right," he said. They sat for a long time without talking. What did you say if you didn't want to break things apart even more or invite a stream of gratingly banal apologies or emit some inhuman howl, Caroline thought. She said nothing. Finally William got up and went to the kitchen for another bottle of wine. She felt him move past her, parting the air with his large frame, heard the creak of the swinging door that they always forgot to oil, the refrigerator door opening, every sound a slap against the silence. He came back and filled her glass, a hand on her head as he passed, the lightest brush. He sat back down.

"I don't want to lose you," he said.

"What do you expect me to do?" she said.

"Try to be patient," he said. "Give me a little time if you possibly can."

"I'll try," she said, getting up, feeling at once heavy limbed and free-floating, both, her body at odds with itself, fighting the knowledge of what it already knew.

"Caroline," he said, as she pushed the door into the kitchen, "Katie doesn't know anything. I want you to know that."

"No, she wouldn't," her mother said. "Our daughter is a little too self-absorbed to pick up on . . ."

"I mean," he said, interrupting her, "we've been very . . ."

"Careful," she finished for him.

Caroline went to bed and watched the moon through the arms of the old magnolia tree outside the window. William stayed downstairs for hours it seemed, finally tiptoeing in and lying, as lightly as possible, beside her. In the darkest part of the night, as they both pretended to sleep, he put a hand on her shoulder and she left it there because she didn't know what else to do, because she was already thinking ahead to the nights when he wouldn't be there.

Their routines went on. She rose, showered, dressed. He did the same. They handed sections of the newspaper back and forth at breakfast, though nobody read anything out loud. There was no noise, no usual William noise. They went to work. She'd agreed to run the inner-city foundation she'd been working for so her days were full and long. He still called once or twice a day from his office, but she suspected he was trying to call when he thought she might be out: lunch, late afternoon when they had their staff meetings. He knew when the meetings were. She knew he knew. The messages were cryptic: "Just me. I'll be home around eight."

And he was home, almost always, for dinner, but he didn't make a move in bed, though they still slept together, sleep sleep.

"Do you want me to go into Steven's room?" he said at one point.

She said: "I don't know. No. I don't know."

"If you do, just tell me," he said.

It was all chillingly civil. Another woman, Caroline thought, would scream, yell, throw things. She knew wives who had. She knew wives who, when confronted by the specter—or rather reality—of another woman, bought new nightgowns or underwear, but the idea felt obscene to her, false, a pathetic pretend beginning. See, I'm a new woman, I will do it differently. Peeky boo, I see you. She couldn't do it. There were no sex tricks to be played here, no underwear to be upgraded. That's not what this was about and she knew it. Her husband was no womanizer, no skirt-chaser, no pathetic middle-aged man salivating after a woman half his age, his daughter's age, his daughter's friend. Of course he was. But it was worse: this, she knew, was a man in love. She wanted to hate him and some days she managed, a fine, crisp autumnal hatred that matched the actual seasonal shift from summer. Mostly she was gnawed by a malevolent sorrow, which, with acute determination, she kept lidded. She moved outside herself and lived beside the sorrow. And waited. For something—or someone—to break.

Katie came home, tan and full of stories. She filled the house with them, even tried to replicate some of Steven's meals for her parents.

"Come, Caroline," William said, almost lightheartedly, "you gotta see this. Our daughter's in the kitchen."

Katie's friends came and there was a respite from the strange suspended state in which they had been living. They had friends over, went to movies, helped Katie move her things into a new apartment nearer downtown, where she was joining a law firm right after taking the bar. She'd moved out before, when she went to college, so to her this was no big thing. For her parents it was different.

"Hey, what's with you guys?" she said to them one afternoon, noting, as they all knelt on the floor of her bedroom packing her books, that this suddenly did seem like a big thing. "You can't pull this empty-nest shit now. You had your chance."

She laughed. William joined her, enough to distract her from measuring her parents' premonition of loss. That night they had a going-away party for her, their friends, her friends. She already had a couple of pals from her new firm in tow, a roundish, tousled-hair woman and a small aggressive blonde with big tortoise-shell glasses. April's name never came up. Katie, in her pragmatic, garrulous way, had moved on and rounded up new suspects. William wore, at Kate's insistence, the tropical shirt she'd brought him from Miami.

"You look ridiculous," Caroline said, a rare smile, as they bumped into each other in the kitchen.

"I am ridiculous," he said without smiling.

With Katie gone and Steven staying in Miami, the house went quiet again. It was like a set with the actors offstage. Caroline pretended they were back in college, roommates in some generic rental house, no attachments to the things around them or each other. It made it easier. She came and went, he came and went. Dinner degenerated into sandwiches eaten together in front of the TV or singly in different rooms. Driving down the freeway through the fall mornings, things a little cooler each day though the sun continued to shine, she thought it odd how one adapts to things, how she would have said just six months earlier, when asked if she could live this way, beside William but not with him, knowing he was seeing someone else—what a wholly inadequate phrase that was: are you seeing someone?—impossible, absolutely impossible. She read about people in prison and prison camps making the necessary adjustments not to go mad, finding new routines in the deprivation. It made sense, survival instincts being what they are. But those people were locked up. She was remaining here of her own volition and daily, hourly, she gyrated between thinking that her tenacity was an act of courage or an act of cowardice. She made a silent promise that if she started hating herself—instead of him and the girl—she would leave. And as the days went by, the nights coming earlier and earlier, the holidays on the horizon, she began shifting closer and closer to the idea of leaving. But it was William who broke first.

"I can't stand this any longer," he said one morning at breakfast, a big guttural sob coming up out of him. "It's destroying us."

Caroline looked over his bent head out the window, mentally checking the weather, bidding herself sit still, sit still, give no comfort, tip no hand. Destroying "us." That's what he'd said. Presumably that included the girl, too. He was still out there somewhere in limboland, wrestling. That she knew. He'd been losing weight. There were dark circles under his eyes now and at night he'd often rise and pace the house. She would hear him at night and in the morning often find him, head in hands, half asleep in his office or passed out on Steven's bed. Katie's room he never ventured into. Too close to the bone. She had no doubt his pain was real. She had no desire to add to it or subtract from it. That would put it—and them—back in the old marital vocabulary. They'd be in it together. And she didn't want that. They weren't together. This was his hand to play, though sitting there, she was tempted, some part of her was, to go to him and hold his head. But she kept her seat, shackled her empathy, in part, yes, because in comforting him, she might somehow be pardoning him, moving him along in his deliberations, and in part because she wasn't sure whether, holding him, her hands near his face, she wouldn't be tempted to rake her fingernails down the tear tracks on his face. But the blood might be therapeutic for him, perversely absolving. So she said nothing, her focus determinedly out the window. There would be no scenes, not on her part. And she wouldn't play that part in his scenes—the hurt and angry wife. She wouldn't let him make her a cliché. She was that, no doubt, but she'd be damned if she'd let him make her sound like one. No, he was going to have to play the scenes by himself.

"Maybe I should go away," he finally said.

"OK," she said.

"I don't mean for a long time. I mean this weekend. To sort this out."

Again he said: "This is destroying us." Again she let the "us" hang there. He might have been talking about them, Caroline and William Betts, but he might not have. He might have been talking about him and the girl or about all three of them. It was not an elucidation Caroline wanted.

"OK," she said, about the weekend. "Maybe it is a good idea."

When he looked up at her, his bloodshot eyes, the dark circles, it was all she could do to walk out of the room.

He left very early Saturday morning. He'd somehow packed out of her sight, or at least thrown whatever stuff he was taking into a duffel bag and already put it in the car, because there was no fiddling to be seen, either Friday night or that morning. Of course, Caroline stayed in bed, turned on her side, pretending sleep as he rose to leave. Doors closing, ever so quietly being pulled to: a husband leaving. Maybe on a fishing trip with buddies. William hating the fishing—"The most boring sport known to man," he'd said—but loving the camaraderie. Maybe taking Steven on a camping trip with his Boy Scout troop, the two departing before dawn, full of high spirits in their matching khaki uniforms. Or catching an early plane to take Katie to look at colleges. William had loved those trips, he and Katie—on the evenings they returned—analyzing the pros and cons of the colleges they'd visited with the determination of generals analyzing battle strategy, making endless lists over dinner and on into the night. Or maybe leaving to take both children, when they were still little, to visit their grandparents, a long car ride, all of them packed in there with dolls and baseball mitts and books—her intrepid trio of road gypsies backing out of the driveway, stopping within an hour to call home from a gas station, one or the other of the kids crying and saying, "Mommy, I miss you," William chiming in, "me too, me too"—the best of all worlds, all those protestations of love coming through the phone while she, back in bed, was lying there luxuriating in the rare quiet of the house.

This, with its intimation of permanence, was a wholly different quiet. Caroline lay very still, as if something, some part of her, might shatter if she moved. The day was just lightening, the branches of the tree becoming visible, the highest branches gilded by the first sun. That's the problem with California, Caroline thought. Bad things happened on the most beautiful days. Hearing a plane in the distance, she realized she had no idea where he was going, whether, in fact, he was taking a plane or just going to some motel in the valley. She had no doubt the girl was going with him and imagined, in as scant detail as she could manage, their tear-stained sex. Or maybe he was farther along than she thought. Maybe there would be no tears. Maybe they were flying up to San Francisco to apartment hunt. Three-quarters of her said no, that scenario didn't gibe with his recent behavior. But one-quarter of her was preparing itself for that. Or that one-quarter was beginning to prepare the other three-quarters so that when he walked in the door Sunday night and said, I'm leaving, she would be ready. Was such a thing possible, that she could be ready for that? She was fooling herself and she knew she was fooling herself, but the preparation for that scene could help get her through the weekend. If she allowed herself to think of the reverse, of him coming home and saying, I'm here, I'm not going, it's over, she would never make it through the weekend. That would leave her with too much to feel.

Katie, luckily, was out of town. Both Caroline and William had navigated around their daughter's growing concern with determined skill, ducking, weaving, avoiding dinners with her, pleading work. Katie would say: "You guys are no fun anymore. What's wrong?" For the most part, she'd been saying it lightly, taken up with her own new job and new friends, but there was an undercurrent of burgeoning worriment that was real and that Caroline figured, without asking, was further tearing at William. The last thing he wanted was for his daughter to find out. The last thing Caroline wanted was for their daughter to find out. In this she and William were co-conspirators. Caroline knew that if Katie found out, she would hate her father, and that might release him to go. It was her love that would help keep him. So the two of them, without acknowledging what they were doing, tiptoed around their sharp-eyed but self-absorbed daughter whose wails of betrayal would not be circumspect and private the way Caroline's would be. Caroline knew those potential wails resounded in William's calibrations and while she hated him for part of that—for letting Katie be a major deciding factor in whether he left her, Caroline—she was also, she had to admit, grateful for her daughter's pull on her father's heart.

So what did you do with such a weekend as this? Were there any guidelines for it? Caroline was not a pill taker nor a real drinker. The occasional sleeping pill and some glasses of wine—that was it. Throwing them at this, trying to fog over the reality, would, she figured, backfire, leaving her in a muzzy, sentimental fog, where more memories would have their way with her. Better to get through it cold. But what literally to do. No kids. No friends. Everyone off limits. She was a prisoner of her secret. All right, she would take it out somewhere, her secret, out to lunch, shopping. Problem was the idea of food was gagging and the idea of standing, half-naked, in some dressing room, looking at her fortysomething body with its courageous pretense of vanity when she knew damn well all it wanted to do was slink to the floor in a fetal curl, was repellent. Be cruel to prop it up and make it perform when in every curve and crevasse of it there was a specific and graphic sense of abandonment, as if the parts themselves—hands, crotch, armpits—were each registering the loss, singing their own individuated lamentations. It got so she couldn't lie there one more minute and listen. She left the bed, grabbing clothes, dressing swiftly, finally, while brushing her teeth, coming up with a plan. She would browse the real estate ads, circle them and spend the next two days visiting open houses, driving, if need be, from one end of the city to the other. Motion, action. She thought it would work. If she couldn't try on clothes, she could try on new lives— a condo on the beach, a rustic aerie in the hills. She would visit them all, trying on personas and lifestyles with each one. She was quite giddy with the solution and bolted out of the house before she could reconsider, driving out the driveway without looking back, already pretending that she had just visited the day's first open house. Nice enough, good rooms if a little shopworn, a lot of dinged-up wood paneling everywhere, obviously some family had lived there, kids grown, maybe a divorce. Too much for a single woman. She'd find something smaller, simpler, newer, something as completely different as her life would be when on Sunday night her husband came home and announced that their twenty-seven-year marriage was at an end.

She began in the hills. The signs were out everywhere: OPEN HOUSE: 220 LAUREL TERRACE. OPEN HOUSE, 130 CHEROKEE LANE. She realized she wouldn't even need the paper much. She could follow the arrows, a kid's game. Fifteen years later, lying in her hospital cot, still sweaty and unnerved by her dream, Caroline remembered everything, every house and apartment and condo she visited that weekend and in what order. So determinedly had she focused on the task at hand, the task of avoidance, that she even remembered, with accuracy, some of the wallpapers and floor coverings. In the first house, a dark, little cabin smack up against a hillside, a fiercely peppy young female broker with masses of dark hair and hoop earrings followed her around like a puppy, extolling the property's virtues.

"They just put in this kitchen. It's small but you know, if you come from New York (so that was the accent) like me it's huge. And did you see the loft off the second bedroom? You can stash a kid or (looking hard at Caroline) a grandkid up there. Is that . . . are you looking at it for yourself?"

"Yes, just me," Caroline said brightly. "My husband's leaving me for another woman." A pause in the patter. She'd stopped the young woman cold.

"I'm sorry," Caroline said.

"Me too," the broker said, her act momentarily deflated and Caroline felt bad. She was going to have to do better than this. But as she left, the woman had recovered.

"This would be a cozy place, you know, for someone like you," she said cheerfully.

"Someone being dumped, you mean," Caroline said cheerfully back.

She dropped by a couple more dark, dank little places with hanging macramé planters and stained-glass windows, making her way up the hillsides, weaving in and out of the side lanes, the sun growing stronger and warmer as the day went along and she rose higher up through the canyons with their inescapable patina still of hippie days. At the tops, there were newer, white-stucco places, crowning jewels with fabulous views of the city and ocean and white carpets and white marble bathrooms and huge front doors. She'd ascended from the '60s up to the shiny, new 1980s. A whole different breed of broker predominated up here in the full sun; young men, ingratiating and clean and of undetermined sexuality. There was about them a very asexual flirtatiousness. They were cooler in their demeanor, didn't dog Caroline's steps, but seemed to materialize at odd points when she turned around.

"Great view, isn't it? See, you can see Catalina (a stab to the heart, Caroline remembering camping trips with the kids, now thinking, maybe that's where they went). And did you see the master closet. Big enough . . ."

"For a family of four," Caroline smilingly finished for him. That was the house right at the top of Mulholland, with its massive stilts.

"Are you OK?" the scrubbed and androgynous young broker said, once again appearing out of nowhere at her elbow.

"Yeah," she said, "I'm just admiring the view," looking at him to see what he was seeing in her. "I'm fine really, thanks. I'll have to bring my boyfriend back. Maybe later today."

"Great," the young man said. "I'll be here 'til five. Here's my card."

Better. The boyfriend part worked for everyone. It had optimism. In the next place, a huge new mansion in Trousdale, she told the middle-aged blonde woman who was showing her around that she had to bring her new husband and their five kids back—her two, his three—and in the smaller place after that, in the flats of Beverly Hills, told an aggressive, pudgy young man that she was really looking at the house for her brother and his, ahem, lover. She was on a roll, zigging and zagging through the streets, dropping her fabrications here and there. The day was unaccountably warm for late fall. She hoped William had left the city so he was not able to warm himself in this, her, sunshine. She wanted him somewhere else. She didn't want him sharing the sun. She played on into the late afternoon, making her way to the beach, stopping at three different houses in Santa Monica, the last a small white architectural box with glass doors everywhere that led to small, pebbly plots with quiet fountains and tucked-away chairs. That stopped her. She could actually imagine herself, alone, here. Alone, by herself, here, a middle-aged divorcee with two grown kids. There was a small second bedroom with a pull-out sofa. One or the other kid could come for quality-time sleepovers. Everyone was grown. They didn't need to nest anymore. This would do. A soft-spoken Asian woman was handling the house, typecast for it, she quiet, it quiet, everybody tasteful and restrained. Caroline suddenly realized they had all been typecast for their houses, the brokers, matched up, agent to property as if by some cosmic real estate match-maker. To this one in this house she gave no line.

"I could live here," Caroline said simply.

"I know," the woman said, "I could, too."

After that, the game ran out of her. She roused herself as the sun went down over the Pacific to tell one more whopper to one last bro-ker, an all grown-up beach boy in khakis and short-sleeved Hawaiian shirt with major white teeth.

"I don't know," Caroline said, looking around the multilevel wood and glass house overlooking the marina, "where I'd put the orphans."

"How many do you have?" he said.

"Five right now, but I'm getting a couple more older ones from Korea."

"Wow," he said. "I've always thought of this as a couples house, but, hey, anything that turns you on."

"Well," she said, "I'll bring them back next weekend, providing lightning doesn't strike for you before that."

"OK," he said with his cheerful and practiced professionalism, knowing full well he would never see her again.

She had been valiant, energetic, but felt soiled as the lies grew larger and she was actually trying to snag somebody's sympathy. Cheap stuff. No more orphans. She'd go back to the new boyfriends and new husbands if she did this again tomorrow. First there was a night to get through. Food was still troubling, as was the thought of going home. It would be dark. She'd forgotten to leave a light on. Maybe there'd be a message on the machine, but she doubted it and didn't want one anyway for fear of what it might say. She hadn't thought this through, but now realized she couldn't go home. She'd have to stay on the loose. A movie, a motel, but there she'd be sitting and that was dangerous. Better just keep moving for a while. She turned the car around and headed back south on Lincoln, passing a rash of new minimalls with Thanksgiving decorations—plastic turkeys and pilgrims—hanging in shop windows. She knew you were supposed to hate these drive-in malls because they were ugly, squat, bereft of any design, but she secretly rather liked them. They were California writ small, serving up perfectly passable fast food in every complexion from Chinese to Mexican to Salvadoran. William liked them, too. Sometimes, they'd get in the car and just graze through a handful of them, trying falafel one place, pupusas the next, beers everywhere. The restaurants were clean and cheerful, redolent of foreign smells and hard work. William didn't have a snobby bone in his body. Quite the reverse. And he'd taught her, brought her along. Not that she was prone to any prejudice, she'd just, growing up in the middle of the state, never been exposed to much. He exposed her, all right, every piece and part of her. Was that the point, that he now needed to do that with some young someone else? Was it that basic— that at a certain point a man just needed or wanted to start over, to have a new conquest, a new body beside him, a new audience for his old stories? As much that as the sex. She hated it, hated him, but she understood it on some level, at least the person that she had temporarily become, this strange free-floating, lie-telling, chipper survivor, understood it. A couple of her friends had lost husbands to younger women, the same friends who had tried crotchless panties and wept bitter, remonstrative tears when they didn't work, Caroline holding them as they cried out in X-rated language about their husbands' need for younger pussy, crying out, too, she thought, for the self-inflicted sexual contortions they'd put themselves through—sucking in their pregnancy-softened stomachs and prancing around lewdly in antic and ill-fated efforts to fend off the new, firmer competition. Not for her. Oh no. If one was going to be left, one didn't want to be left with such images of oneself.

She rolled down the windows and turned the heat on full heading toward the airport. She was tempted by a number of airport motels, figuring their bars would be full of noise, passengers, pilots. But stopping still felt too dangerous and she didn't really want to drink. It wouldn't help. It would just do the reverse: let the defenses down. Better to keep moving, see if she could wear herself out at least a little before settling down somewhere for the night. There were stars and a citrus wedge of a moon. The night had cooled considerably. Saturday night. People were out, going to movies, malls, restaurants. She passed a couple of big empty lots full of rotting pumpkins left from Halloween, banners already up advertising the Christmas trees to come. Everything was a beacon of tradition, a familial prompt, arrows pointing down memory lane. But she'd become a taskmaster with her own heart. The cardiac hatches were battened down. She passed a series of brightly lit car lots, a couple of customers still talking to salesmen, and figured if she couldn't manage more houses she could always drive cars tomorrow, though on the chain, real estate agents were more manageable than car salesmen. They'd leave you alone if you made them. A beige stucco motel caught her eye: Oceanside Cottage, its sign read, with a picture of an Englishy cottage and underneath: WATER BEDS AND X-RATED MOVIES. A perfect mixed metaphor. William would have loved it. Caroline was actually able to smile, a real smile, not the sharp, fake ones she'd turned on the various real estate brokers like a syrupy slap. The realness of it unloosed something in her and before she could regroup, the tears came. Unbidden, big and silent, and she could not stop them now that they had started nor the image of her husband's ass in the air—he had taught her to say that word and the others, not liking, he said emphatically, the coy substitutes—as he crooningly fucked, maybe on a water bed, sloshing up and down, a pretty, dark-haired young woman that their very own daughter had brought home for his delectation. Up and down his ass went in front of Caroline's flooded eyes, up and down, up and down, up and down, and she pulled over and around the corner into a residential side street and rolled up the windows and locked the doors and, finally tearless, fell asleep.

She woke, cold and achy, and uncertain for a moment where she was—a deserted residential street. Generic street, generic suburb. It was still dark. She started the engine and saw it was 3:30. This was one way to get through a night. She marveled at how unhinged you could get and how fast. Here she was sleeping in her car. Was this a harbinger or just a one-shot? She didn't know. One of the perverse dividends of being in crisis, she realized, is that you had no fear. You were beyond it. Here she'd fallen asleep in her car and waking in the dark didn't even think of being frightened. The idea of someone breaking in and stabbing her or raping her didn't hold any weight. It was silly, meaningless, beside the point. Real terror lay elsewhere, closer to home, at home. Sooner or later, sooner than later, she'd have to go back there, but not yet, not 'til it was light. She had another couple of hours to kill. Maybe she could eat now. She felt calm again, her body not yet arched up with vigilance. Time to get some food in it—or try to. She pulled back out onto Lincoln heading north, a few cars coming and going from the airport, the occasional limousine. In the mini-malls, the twenty-four-hour convenience stores were still open, but the restaurants were closed. She put her window down and the ocean smell was strong, reviving. Maybe it would all be OK, whatever that meant. What did it mean? She inhaled deeply of the chilly, salted air and felt a sweet, aberrant pang of hunger. Appetite. Appetites. Survival. Near Pico, she pulled into an all-night coffee shop with a huge penguin in black tie smiling down from the roof. The kids had always loved it. She would eat their food: pigs in a blanket. And drink coffee and read the Sunday paper and, fortified, make her way home. She actually got them down, two pigs, two sausages swaddled in a doughy pancake, 'til her body awoke and went back on the alert and that was it for the eating. But she stayed on, sipping coffee, reading the paper—not reading, pushing it around and looking at it—while the sun came up and stragglers from some black-tie party, no doubt in the Marina, dribbled in, noisy and still high, a couple of middle-aged guys with younger women in long, tight, slinky dresses. She looked out the window, swatches of pink across the slowly brightening sky. Another beautiful day in paradise. That's what it was going to be. That's what William used to say.

"Look," he'd say, pushing open the shutters in their bedroom. "Look at that, another beautiful damn day in paradise," stretching nude and furry in the morning light.

Maybe he would die today. Maybe the plane he was taking back from San Francisco or wherever the hell they'd gone would fall from the sky and shatter in a million pieces, blowing his body to bits—and hers—so the future would not hold these bouncy, ebullient, naked images. She would be free of them. He would be free of her. She would be the best widow, comforting her grieving children, never letting on that the girl's happening to be on the plane with William was anything but a coincidence. In her profound and exacting grief—why did it happen, how did it happen, who's responsible—Katie would certainly find April's name among the list of passengers. But Caroline would stay mum. She would be graceful and beneficent to the end. She would let him die loved. Was it too much to hope for, too much to ask for? One itty-bitty plane crash.

She drove home through quiet Sunday streets, down along the oceanside bluffs. The palm trees stood sentry, even rows of them, their fronds crackling in the slight breeze. Another beautiful day in paradise. It was already warm, another of those sun-bathed autumn days, another day to get through. No more house tours, no cars, no manic flapping around. She had done that. Maybe after cleaning up, she would come back down here and take a walk or go to a movie. She drove up San Vicente with its wide center strip and signature coral trees. There were a few joggers already out. Later the strip would be clogged. It was all still dreamy right now, as pretty a street, Caroline thought, as any in the world. Around the bend by the Veteran's Hospital and by the cemetery with its row after row of little white markers—yes, he could die today; why not?—and then a few more turns and she was, inescapably, ineluctably, in sight of her house, her driveway, and no, he wasn't there, his car wasn't. She knew then how badly she'd been hoping for it, not daring to hope in a conscious place. But hope it had been, the huge stupid hope that her errant husband would be there where he belonged. Of course he would be there, repentant, flowers in hand. Of course he wouldn't. She sat in her car for a long time looking at the house. It could use a paint job, certainly if it was going to be put up for sale. The pale yellow had browned, the shutters were slightly peeling. Yard still looked pretty good. A family home. Perfect for kids. Within walking distance of the public schools—not that anyone who could afford to move into this neighborhood now would actually send their kids there. Hers had gone to them but that was in another lifetime.

She finally was able to go in. She went directly up the stairs to start the bath, the house chilly and dark still, bypassing with determination the kids' rooms, the pictures in the hall and, most treacherous, the answering machine in the bedroom. What if he had simply called and said: I'm not coming home. Not like him. The coward's way out.

But none of this was like him. She soaked for a long time, making the water hotter and hotter, washing her hair, not looking down at her body. She covered herself quickly with a towel, avoiding the bathroom mirror. Dressed in casual Sunday clothes, jeans and a pink pullover, tennis shoes, she finally went and sat on the bed and stared at the machine. Three, it said, and she inhaled deeply. She closed her eyes and pressed. A hang-up. A call from Steven in Miami, sweet and oblivious: "Hi Mom, hi Dad, love you, I'll try you tomorrow." Two down and one to go. Beep: a scratchy noise, airplane noise, it sounded like, and her heart jumped, then through the gargle, Katie, somewhere with lousy reception. "Hey guys, thought we might catch dinner tonight. I'm coming back around six. I'll call back." There it was: all family members accounted for. Except one. Maybe that was the hang-up. Couldn't dwell on that or you'd go crazy. Right now, there was a day to get through, crawl through. She needed to get away from the house, the nonringing of the phone, the non-everything. Out. But where? Where did you go when you had nothing to do and how could you have nothing to do when just the other day, the other month, you had everything to do. Everything so full—the calendar, the refrigerator, the driveway. Now everything was suspended. It was like the time she waited for the results of a biopsy, a long, plucky day when fear had its way with you and you fought it off, time and again, minute by minute, hour after hour: it will be, it won't be, it will be, it won't be, fear, reprieve, fear, reprieve, fear, reprieve. But he'd been there with her then, coming home from lunch, making her drink the red wine he'd stopped to buy, taking her to bed.

"Who needs this?" he said, gently touching her breast, careful to avoid the Band-Aid over the small incision. "The important stuff is still here,"—his hand cupping her crotch. He was being literal, leering, trying to make her laugh. He put her hand around his erection, but it went soft. He couldn't do it either and she smiled at him because she knew he was scared, too. They lay in the afternoon together, drifting, drinking more, 'til the phone rang and with the good news, he whooped and squishing her breasts together took both nipples in his mouth at once.

"You phony," she said, ruffling the top of his head. "You love these things. You men are all the same."

Venice on a warm, fall afternoon. It was noisy, raffish, aromatic. The smell of deep-fried corn dogs competed with the scents of salty air and peppery-sweet incense. Caroline made herself breathe it all in, anchoring herself to the smells, the boardwalk pageantry. She had friends who were scared to come down here—still now in the early '80s—but William hooted at that and his bravado had given her bravery. Anyway, this is not where you got hurt, among sleazy T-shirt vendors and aging hippies with guitars and incipient beer guts. Hardly where you got hurt. The noise ebbed and flowed—the sunglass hawkers, the radios, the gang kids with their tattoos and X-rated patois, swaggery street toughies often with marshmallow insides. Caroline knew the breed well from her work. Scratch the armor, whatever color it came in—white, black, brown—and you found a generic kid. She thought of her own. They were tough enough themselves to survive the breakup of their parents. At least half of their friends had already gone through it. This came with an extra fillip of betrayal—the girl and all. But kids survived. Even Kate would come around at some point, wouldn't she? She saw them, Stevie and Kate, chummily smiling down at their new half sibling, an infant in William's arms, and had to sit suddenly, blinking hard against the image of her own exile. If she'd had anything in her stomach, it would not have stayed down.

"You all right?" A girl had stopped, a black girl with a thousand braids and huge gold hoops in her ears. She came into focus. "You were kinda mumbling and shaking."

"All right," Caroline said, flatly, looking blankly at her.

"Sorry," she said tartly. "I didn't mean to bother you."

"No," Caroline said. "Thanks." She smiled. She felt the smile out there on her face but it had nothing to do with her.

"Sure," the girl said, spinning fast back into the parade ranks on her skates, leaving Caroline there. She'd slept in her car and now she was mumbling on a public bench. The lines were thin, weren't they, she thought. You could tumble into the nutty never-never land pretty easily, it turned out. Even Caroline Betts with her combed hair and pressed jeans could do that and that was something to know—all those years of feeling grounded, grounded in love, by love, gone, the ground itself gone with the love. You could get unhinged pretty quickly it turned out, everything up for grabs, even your hold on reality—especially if that's what you didn't want to hold on to. She understood now clearly something she had not quite articulated to herself: that this had to be over tonight, one way or the other. If he wanted more time, she did not have that to give.

She remembered a little Mexican place at the far end of the boardwalk and decided to go try a margarita, passing on her way the crowd around the man juggling the live chain saw, throwing it up and catching it backhand as it whirred away, teeth bared. William hated it, the deliberate courting of disaster in a public place. He got unexpectedly gruff the first time they saw it. She was miffed, smiled at him.

"Come on," she said, "it's like a circus act."

"I didn't come out here to go to the circus," he said. "There's enough real wreckage around here"—she was caught off guard sometimes by his seriousness because the grin was always hovering. She didn't mind the chain saw, found it kind of witty, in fact. She preferred anything to animal tricks, didn't think animals ought to be conscripted into human follies. She'd refused to go when he took the kids to Sea World in San Diego, a thousand years ago. They'd all begged her to come, but no. See, she did have it: resolve. She could draw her lines.

The margarita was cold, huge, translucent, the salt thick and gummy around the rim of the glass. She sat in a roped-off bar at the edge of the beach with her bare feet in the sand, toes digging down below the surface warmth. It was fall. Her toes knew it. The sand was cold just below the surface. The sun was still hot on her arms, but the tiniest sea breeze lifted up the edges of the heat. The hot spell was beginning to break. By tomorrow or the next day, temperatures would be back to normal for this time of year. She would live in those days, whatever happened. But there would be something new about her. Whatever happened. That, too, she understood. You didn't get this far out of your own life and just slip back in unnoticed if indeed it was still there for you to slip back into. She saw her daughter's sweet, sharp, no-nonsense gaze, her gabardine shoulders, her lawyer's mouth, her garrulous, bristly, overachieving daughter. What did Katie know of forgiveness? She got out of her own marriage with a stunning, feminist-tinged matter-of-factness, but this, her parents' marriage, would be wholly different. Caroline would have to help her, help them both, though she wasn't worried about Steven. He was hers; he'd take her lead. If she wanted William forgiven, Steven would do that. And she would have to want that. That's what abandoned wives were supposed to want, certainly if there were children, even grown ones like hers. There were ethics, Caroline thought, even in abandonment. She would be exacting with herself and with them, her children, expecting them to behave well, allowing them even to love those sure-to-come half siblings. They would not, as other families had done, act out in public, make scenes—scream, sue, rant. She would not let them dishonor themselves that way—dishonor her. She would be elegant, restrained, magnanimous in her abandonment, an example to all. William would be grateful—weighed down with gratitude. Not guilt. She would not allow him the perverse pleasure of guilt. But gratitude, yes. It would bounce along behind him—his deep and desperate gratitude—like those tethered tin cans bouncing along behind the marriage getaway car, *clink, clank, clink, clank, clink, clank.* A reminder. By her magnanimity she would not be forgotten—or pitied. Her enduring grace would remind him of her, of how she made his new life, his new family possible. She would be an example to all! Fuzzy with tequila—though these things never tasted like they had much in them, but then again she hardly ever drank hard liquor—she warmed to the image of her later self, lean, elegant, spare of sex and rancor. The perfect first wife. Content with the image, she leaned down and rested her cheek on the warm tabletop, just for a minute because it had looked so inviting, and who would notice here—the first drunks were raising their voices now, things getting rowdy in the late sun, she heard them, a few guys arguing about some game, baseball ("That stupid pitcher." "Shit, you don't know your ass from baseball.") but it got farther away as she drifted toward a soft sleep, sun-warmed and tequila-warmed, the tawny rump of Catalina looking like a slumbering animal out there on the horizon line, close and soft enough to stroke. This would be fine, if she could only stay here, like this, drifting in the sun . . . her noble, sleepy self drifting . . .

She must have drifted off because when she woke, she was stiff and cold on her small cot, the window still open above her. She knew where she was. She didn't always, waking here, was sometimes completely disoriented for the time it took the ventilator noise to penetrate. But this time she came to easily. The dawn light came through the window above her head. Another day. One more sweet, long, mute day. It was all right—a kind of a life and they were still sharing it. Of course, there was always a chance something would change. Maybe today was the day.

She heard the carts clattering down the hall—food for those who could still eat. A kind of bland, congealed smell drifted in. She turned her head away toward the wall, wondering when she would be hungry again, how long it would take after this: how many months. She was hungry with Steven, rather hungry for him, to make him happy, but there was no real hunger. It was that odd feeling she remembered—as if she had left her own body. It was here, soldiering on, eating, going to the bathroom, preening even. Oh yes, she was shining her carapace— the makeup, the hair. It was a useful exercise. It clearly amused and alarmed the children but it deflected them, gave her room. It also deflected the concern of the various do-goodnicks who came through the door with their bromides about taking care of yourself. She seems to be doing that—our Caroline. She's amazing. So strong. Well, you know, she's always been like that.

She rose to pee, stopping by William on the way to the bathroom, leaning to kiss his eyelids, first one then the other. Not real kisses. She flicked the tip of her tongue across one and then the other, hoping still, against all signs and scans to the contrary, to conjure a flutter. She'd sell her soul for a flutter. But they were cool, his eyelids, and totally calm as they had been since he came here and she wondered, with a bolt of envy, about the other dramas down the hallways where the dying were still lucid, if pain-filled, where conversations and non-conversations could be had or not had. Not for them. Not for him. It had been total noise one moment, then total silence the next. That's what had happened. There was no sliding off, no lowering of the deci-bel level. And she knew in her bones as she reached for him across the breakfast table that morning three weeks ago, he in mid-oration as usual, suddenly stopping and looking odd and slumping forward, that that was so and that he would not again speak, devoutly as, in here, in the weeks after, she had tried to unremember that.

In the bathroom, she was amused by her roots. They were already showing, a thin band of telltale gray around her forehead. No wonder she hadn't done this. It required real attention. You had to stay on the case. It gave her a mission. Monday's mission. Color the roots. Her friends had long been doing it and that's what they said. I've got to get my roots done. Now she had belatedly joined their ranks and would leave the hospital with this if nothing else: a new phrase, a new habit. She would want those.

She did her hair, standing for a long time in the shower, some of the residual dye streaking her body and running into her pubic hair. Were you supposed to dye that, too? Who were you fooling? She smiled to herself—at herself. She dressed, a simple blue sweater, clean khakis, and waited for the girl to come so she could take her walk. She straightened the room, spruced up her cot, plumping pillows, fixing the flowers that had come. She had scissors, gardening gear by now, a neat little box on the window sill, and was fully equipped to cut, trim, rearrange, eliminating the dead flowers and making new bouquets out of the still vibrant ones. She trimmed the African daisies and changed the water in the vases, moving to and from the bathroom—William there in the middle—walking around the foot of the bed again and again, throwing away clippings, around and back and forth. She didn't hum, had never been a hummer, or talk to herself, or have any temptation to turn on a radio or TV. It was the ventilator she wanted to hear, needed to hear. That was the background music for this new life of theirs. *Sshhh-pft, sshhh-pft, sshhh-pft.*

The first of the specialists came—a young female pulmonary specialist with heavy dark hair and big gold hoop earrings. Mondays were like this. They all came, one after the other. Their egos refreshed from the weekend (From what? Caroline wondered, studying them one by one as they bounced in. From weekend sex or tennis triumphs or cocktail-party contact with genuflecting civilians?), they entered cheerfully, made modest small talk, read the chart, and bounced out. No change, they said, in variations of doctor speak. By now she wasn't expecting any. There'd been a flurry of hope in the beginning, brain scans still hopeful, but in the past two weeks, just this. No change. He could linger. It was up to her now. But still they came back, adding their own diurnal scratches in the chart—the hieroglyphic record of an ebbing life—and went away leaving Caroline Betts once more to her own calibrations, which were the only ones anymore that truly mattered.

The girl she had hired to sit couldn't come 'til the afternoon because of finals. She finally arrived, looking beleaguered and tense.

With a mumbled "Hi," she took her accustomed place in the chair at the foot of the bed and opened her book, releasing Caroline to go. It was always hard—leaving. Something could happen in the brief time she was away. It could. She had to force herself always to cross the threshold and go out into the corridor. She was usually OK once she was out there, although until she was in the elevator she had to fight the temptation to turn back. With her demeanor, she deflected niceties from the families of the other patients, kept her head down as she headed straight for the elevator, careful not to bump into any of the hall trudgers with their rolling IVs, one hand often behind the back trying to keep the gown from flapping open and exposing an aging buttock.

"Jesus," Katie had said, "why can't they get Calvin Klein or somebody to upgrade these things. It's pathetic. At least Wills doesn't have to be out here trying to cover his ass."

"Katie," Steven said, looking around to make sure no one had heard her.

"Don't look if it bothers you," Caroline had said sharply to Katie, slipping out of maternal gear, tenderhearted for a moment about the vanities of the other inmates. She had her own, didn't she? More than that: she would not again hold that "ass," and there walking to the elevator between her two grown, quarrelsome children, she felt a sharp stab of pure pornographic longing, enough to wince audibly, causing her kids to reach out on both sides, Steven putting an arm around her, Katie taking her wrist, and gently steer her into the elevator.

Today she was on her own and she moved swiftly to the elevator and was out of the hospital without having to talk to or really even look at anybody. She'd gotten good at that. The day was warm still, a bit smoggy. She never looked back at the hospital from outside and never, on her walks, strayed near the house. Steven did it, went by and checked the message machine, sorted the mail, dealt with the gardener and the cleaning woman. It was he who had, without being asked, brought the gardening tools. He was like that. He would come later today with dinner, a family dinner in their new home. She was glad Katie wasn't here all the time. Too much noise, too much articulation about things. She dropped stuff off at the cleaners, went and got her sandwich, her coffees, a few magazines—which she knew she wouldn't really read, look at maybe, but not read—and then sat in a shady spot on the campus among the lunchtimers. She made herself come out here because she knew it was important to get away—at least a little, never more than an hour at a time because that was pushing the envelope, tempting fate—from the room and because the coming out made the going back sweeter. He was still there. Coming and going, she was a wife, a woman with a husband, a woman with errands to do. She would live in there with him forever if they'd let her, bringing in her children and her sandwiches and arranging her flowers.

A Frisbee game broke out on the lawn near her, kids stressed by finals forming into ad hoc teams, squeally and sweaty and strong-limbed. There was a small argument about the rules, then laughter and the game resumed. In other clumps, students studied, heads down, shoving food in without even noticing and somebody with a bullhorn tried to rally people to support the farmworkers. That had been going on forever. Things changed and nothing changed. Caroline loved this campus, had from the day she set foot on it. It was so big and open right there in the middle of this big, open city. Everything seemed so vast and promising after her small-town childhood, the great wide lawns, those huge lecture halls with their sloping seats and carved-up desks. She even loved the bad, old days, the late '60s and early '70s when it was a war zone, constant protest marches and sit-ins and people with bullhorns exhorting this or that crowd to join this or that cause. William, in blue jeans, spent late nights at the law school counseling draftees, then brought them home to sleep on the floor, everybody talking and arguing and eating late into the night, the boys scared underneath their bravado—"Nixon's a fuckin' creep," they'd say, or they'd call him "a faggot"—William calming them down, sharing a joint with them. He liked marijuana. He didn't smoke it with his own kids—"I do have my standards," he'd said, laughing—but he did smoke with the kids he brought home and sometimes with their friends—his and Caroline's—the men's hair suddenly silly-long, some growing beards, the women practicing public nudity as they all, of a backyard evening, climbed in and out of the new neighborhood hot tubs. Where did they go, those big old redwood tubs? Did someone just come get them in the dark of night, dragging them all away to some hot tub graveyard or back to some scraggly vineyard from which they had come. They were there one minute, one year, one decade—and then gone the next. Caroline always wore her one-piece black suit and no one gave her grief. They did the first couple of times, but not after the night when William, stripping down, said to the other youngish husbands: "You shmucks don't deserve to see my wife naked," said it lightly, clearing space for her modesty. He, capaciously and easily nude, was garrulous in those tubs, passing the joint, always pushing his thick wet hair this way and that way off his face so it stood up in a dark spiky crown—a big noisy Neptune—everyone leaning in to hear him over the noise of the jets, the women's breasts bobbing toward him on the agitated, moon-splashed water. A couple of their couple friends had slept together—maybe all four at once, certainly two and two. Somehow everyone knew.

"I guess that's part of the thrill," William said derisively, "letting everyone know. It's so corny. I wouldn't be caught dead with someone else's wife. I have my standards." He loved saying that in a self-mocking way, but he always meant it. And, of course, when he finally did sleep with someone else, she was not somebody's wife. And it was not what he dismissively called sport-fucking. And it was already the 1980s and the hot tubs were gone and the war was over and a lot of divorces had already been had among their circle—the couples who had slept together had long since split up. What were their names? The Jepsons, Annie and Mike, but who were the others? William would remember, would have remembered—and some of their kids were already working on their own divorces. It was then that William Betts fell in love with a young woman half his age, a young woman named after a month.

He was there that night she returned from the beach, her mouth still sticky with tequila and salt. She'd stayed away 'til nine, driving up and down the coast in a loopy, controlled panic. Up and down, almost to Oxnard and back to the Marina, killing hours, hands gripping the wheel, passing shacks and mansions packed together, watching the moon on the water. A fog began, harbinger of the end of the unseasonal heat, so that when she finally, at exactly 9:03 P.M., turned onto her own street and looked ahead to her driveway she couldn't be sure she was seeing what she hoped she was seeing: his car. She squinted as she neared the house, driving now as slowly as possible, and indeed it was there: his car. He was home. A searing relief went through her, followed by immediate terror: for how long? Just because he was there didn't mean he was staying. Fear, reprieve, fear, reprieve, fear, reprieve. She crept slowly in her car toward the house and finally stopped without pulling into the driveway. She didn't know why. It was instinctual—a fast getaway car if need be. She sat for a long time. The house was dark. There didn't seem to be a single light on, unless it was way in the interior. He was in there in the dark. Had he made a decision—or would she have to? It seemed unfair, unmanly, unlike him to leave it to her, but who knew. Maybe the young woman had followed him home and he'd left the car and everything, every worldly possession he owned, and just taken off with her. Maybe there was a short, cryptic note in there saying that. She wrestled with that thought and decided no, that he would not do. He was in there, whole or in pieces, resolute or irresolute, the circles under his eyes, she could only imagine, as deep and as dark as she had ever seen them, as they had ever been. She wanted to rush in, turn on all the lights, welcome him home, make a meal, laugh, talk, stroke—as if none of this had happened, was happening, as if there'd been a miscue in the script and they had momentarily been playing someone else's parts. The impulse was so strong that she was at the front door before reality reclaimed her. She stood, in total terror, hand on the doorknob, as if inside there was not her husband but some deranged intruder. She tip-toed in as silently as possible—why, again, she didn't know, some instinct—and gently, gently brought the door to behind her. She stood listening to her house. She didn't hear a sound, save a few whirrings— the refrigerator, an electric clock somewhere. A creak made her start. But there was no human sound at all. Her eyes accustomed to the dark, she walked to the living room. Not there. One room down. To the kitchen, just peaking in and then, ever ever so quietly, to the threshold of his office, covering her mouth quickly, trying to stifle her own sharp intake of breath, when she saw the back of his head. He was sitting behind his desk looking out into the night. Her hatred right then of his big, square, turned-away head was overwhelming. She heard it: her hatred. Did he? Nobody moved. Nobody said anything. She figured he sensed her there. She wanted to scream: talk to me, you coward, tell me, read me my rights. She moved in and sat on the arm of the sofa, just inside the door. And sat. The mechanical whirrings continued. A cat fight broke out outside, causing her to start—that scratchy, high-pitched feline wailing. And then that subsided. How long did they sit so? Finally, without turning toward her, without even turning his head, he said: "I'm home." She said nothing. What could she say: yes, I see. After another long stretch—was he trying to collect himself, trying not to cry?—he added: "For good."

She doubled up there on the sofa arm, but he couldn't see her and she resolutely kept quiet. He would stay. They would go on. A thousand questions hung in the air, a thousand questions unasked and unanswered. Why? Because he loved her so? Or was it only guilt? Could he not bear to hurt Katie? Or had the girl herself made the choice—decided she did not want him, could not do it? She didn't ask that night and she never asked later because she was scared to know. He was home. They would go on.

"It won't happen again," he said after another while, his voice breaking.

She knew he meant it and she knew other women hearing that would have been relieved. But she knew what it meant: this had been the real thing and there was no reason to try it again. He did not leave for this, he would never leave. They would grow old together. They sat for a long time saying nothing, 'til Caroline got up and left the room. She came back and stood in the doorway.

"Don't try to make me feel sorry for you," she said, "because you didn't have the guts to leave me."

She went upstairs in the dark and crawled into Katie's bed with all her clothes on. Neither of them ever again mentioned the girl.

Caroline's beeper went off—a first. She literally jumped, fastidious enough though as always to pick up her trash and toss it in the can as she race-walked to the nearest phone. Out of order. She took off for the hospital, half running, sweaty by the time she got inside to the elevator bank. There were lots of people, a multihued spill of them, a group of Hispanics—the men in dark blue work clothes, their names embroidered over their pockets, the women in pants with kids by the hand, everybody laughing (no doubt a baby or something good happening for them), three serious young men in suits and ties (who knew—a father or brother in trouble), and two young women in saris, their thin gold bracelets clinking as they reached for the elevator button—again and again, everyone impatient. In came a black family—five kids, all ages, noisy, laughing and punching at each other while their parents fought back tears. Caroline herself slipped through the crowd and started pressing the button, but the elevators were still floors away according to the little lighted monitor above them. She went running to the front to find the stairs. Sorry, she was told, there were none available, only for fires or something serious.

"This is serious," she said, losing it, yelling, hearing her own voice rise and feeling powerful behind it. "I can't wait. I'm going up."

A gray-haired woman came around from behind the Information desk and took her arm calmly, authoritatively, but Caroline shook her off and fled back to the elevator bank. The others had all gone, evaporated into their own private dramas. If she had simply stood still, she'd be up there now with the rest of them. She paced, digging her nail into the back of her hand. What if . . . Finally an elevator came and she rushed in, hearing someone say, "Hold it please"—caught in that moment between her customary politeness and abject terror. She punched six and the doors closed without anyone else getting on, so she was uncharacteristically alone—an intimation of widowhood. She got off so intent on getting to the room she actually bumped into the girl coming down the corridor, books held tightly to her chest.

"What?" she almost screamed, scanning her face.

"Your son's here," the girl said nonchalantly.

"My God," Caroline said, "that's all?"

"You told me to call you if anyone came."

"Right," Caroline said, her heart beginning to quiet. "Anyone. OK, thanks. I'll call you later about tomorrow."

She walked slowly to the room, smelling something pungent and curryish and she couldn't help smiling as her heart stopped thudding, knowing Steven was in there doing his thing. His back was turned to her as she reached the threshold of their little nest. She stood still watching him. He was lifting out his cartons and arranging things on the window ledge, definitely Indian food, the smell of cardamom—was that it?—and curry powder, a thick, yellow smell inviting even to someone without hunger. Steven was intent, lifting and spooning and arranging, but when he turned toward the door, hearing his mother, tears were streaming down his soft, round face and she moved swiftly around the end of the bed and held him close.

"Mom," he finally said, "I can't take much more of this."

She didn't say anything for a long time, but she knew he was right. It didn't make sense to go on much longer. They were not going to let her live in here, after all—none of them.

"I'll call your sister and tell her to come. Maybe she can be here Friday. I guess we don't need another weekend in here," she said, face against his shirt. She had just given away her final Sunday.

They ate, but something had finally yielded in Steven and periodically tears would sweep down his face and into his carton of lamb curry.

"You're going to ruin that with all that additional salt," Caroline said, trying to be light.

He tried in turn—engaging her about the two different chutneys, but there was no energy in it. They'd crossed a line. The word had been given. Caroline knew she could not go back on it. And when he left with his bag of aromatic trash, she picked up the phone and called Katie. True to form, she wasn't home, so Caroline left a message.

"There's been no change, sweetie, but you need to come the end of the week. I'd rather have talked to you in person, but I can never find you. Thursday, Friday at the latest, but early Friday. You can call up 'til ten or catch me in the morning. Love you."

So it was all set in motion now—the untethering of William Betts. They had told her how it would be. They would disconnect everything, pull the breathing tube out and he would last only a stretch of hours—three, four, maybe six. It would be peaceful. His breathing would become erratic. His body would cool from the limbs in, saving its heat for the vital organs: brain and heart. And then the heartbeat would slow and finally flatten. She had not told the children, but she would when they were together. No more Sundays. Not one more.

She got ready for bed. A finite amount of nights. Probably four, unless he fooled them and lived on past Friday even after everything had been disconnected. She was facing now a certain eviction. She looked at the flowers, the stacks of books—unread but there—all the homey touches, death chamber by *Metropolitan Home*. Nobody ever said she wasn't a heavy nester.

"Mrs. Betts?" On her cot, Caroline flinched, but saw quickly it was the big, nice night nurse who had comforted her. "Doin' OK tonight?"

"So far," Caroline said, aiming for cheeriness.

"I'll check back on you. You need anything to sleep?"

"I've still got some, thanks."

She hadn't taken a pill yet tonight and was thinking that, from here on in—or out—she wouldn't take anymore. There was so little time.

"What'dya think?" she said softly to her husband. "How's my timing?" She leaned up on an elbow and looked at him—she had an unwritten rule, don't get up and get near him in the night because then she might never be able to pull herself back in. Careful, careful, careful. Your heart could go flying right out of your body through your mouth in an unstoppable wail. She knew the danger. She felt it—had felt it every day since they'd been here. One false move, one nestle too long against William's intubated chest, and she'd be done for. You had to husband yourself (ha, ha), stay calm, stay alert for what you had to do. It was finally officially countdown time. A few more days to live in here with him. A few more days for the girl to make her appearance—in person. Of course she would hardly be a girl anymore, but Caroline knew she would recognize her instantly, even with added years. That's what she'd been waiting for. From the day they'd moved in here, she'd been expecting her to come, to know about William and come find him. No matter how silly or preposterous the notion (she was no doubt miles and memories away by now in her own life), Caroline had not been able to shake it and she wanted to be there in that room when she did come. (Hence the beeper. It was not for William, as everyone assumed. Oh no, she'd fooled them all, had quiet, careful Caroline Betts.) Not only in that room, but looking her best—the hair, the clothes—so she, the other, younger woman, would see that she, Caroline, had not been a consolation prize. She had kept herself up all these years. Not that she wouldn't have done that anyway. She would have, though perhaps not quite so adamantly. She didn't overeat or overdrink—never had. And she and William had exercised. The Centrum Twins on their hikes and bikes—that's what Katie called them. They'd biked through France and walked through Italy and then walked through France and biked through Italy. They'd been to Cairo and Cape Town and Caracas. They'd been everywhere and seen everything and now she wanted the younger woman to come and see them, to bear witness to their happiness before it was over. Come see us. We have been very, very happy. Everyone says so. Just ask anyone.

They groped their way back into a marriage, but it was not the old marriage, it was a new one. The old marriage was gone. William did not bring flowers or tender any apologies and Caroline was relieved. The gestures would have seemed inconsequential, insulting. In front of the children, they were effortful, jocose, William going the extra mile to camouflage what had happened. That first Christmas, coming so quickly on the heels of it all, they kept the house full of friends and noise and then, when everyone had gone of an evening, they went back to their separate bedrooms. William did not say anything. He did not beseech or beckon. The marriage slid sideways, siblingward. Friends.

They were friends, civil, inquiring—How was your day? How was yours?—collegial. It was a new, different kind of limbo than had preceded his weekend away. It didn't have the tension and indecision that that limbo had. This limbo had air in it—a disconnect, a deflation—as if the house were now inhabited by ghosts. In a sense it was: the ghosts of their former selves moving about their big wood-paneled house. Caroline did not know what she was feeling—not entirely. She just wanted to stay quiet, contained, and see if her new self could or would emerge into some kind of facsimile of the old one. She didn't know how long it would take. She didn't know how long it would be before she could again lie down next to her husband. Nor did she know what he was feeling, how damaged was his own heart, and she feared to ask because then she would see, no matter how he tried to camouflage it, the depth of his loss of the girl. She, Caroline Betts, had won. She had prevailed. Her husband had stayed. Hip, hip hooray.

Finally, again, it was William who made the first small moves. He started leaving her small teasing notes outside Katie's bedroom door, where she would find them in the morning. I'm cold. Come back. How about a date? They did make her smile, a smile she was sometimes able to show him across the breakfast table. Her smiles emboldened him. His notes got friskier. No date? OK. How 'bout a jump in the sack? He recognized in her tight smile that morning that he might have overplayed his hand. He backed up. It was like the beginning. He became careful. He circled her, brushing up against her in the kitchen, giving her a soft kiss on the forehead, waiting for her. It was contrary to his instincts, she saw in his eye. He wanted to jump her, bury his body in hers. Their appetites would show them the way out, rather the way back in. His body was on alert, ready, poised. She almost felt stalked. It was eerie, lonesome. She tried, kneeling one night to take his cock in her mouth—two months had passed—but he felt her reticence and it made it feel dirty. For the first time in their lives together. He went limp, made a joke: "This fellatio is fallacious," he said, lifting her head.

"No," she said, "let me go on."

"No," he said, "don't," lifting her head forcibly with both hands. "Stop it."

He said it emphatically. She looked up at him. What, at that moment, she wondered, did he see in her face, poised above his belly. Anger, longing, love? She didn't know. She couldn't feel what was out there on it herself. She smiled a big, broad, fake smile to get her face unstuck from the tight, angry falsity of its sucking pose. He misinterpreted it—or did he? He saw it as malice and permitted himself, for the first time, his own anger.

"Go away," he said, rolling over away from her. "Just get out of here."

Maybe she should have released him to leave her. She knew how to play that part: the wife who'd been left. That she'd figured out. This she didn't know how to play: the wife of the man who'd stayed. She went back to Katie's room.

He said he would go talk to someone with her. But she hated the idea. She didn't want anyone to know—had never told anyone, even her closest friends—not what had happened now, but what it had been like then. The brute, sensate happiness that had been hers so young. Talking about it would trivialize it and he had already done that and she didn't want it to happen anymore. She figured she could find her way back somehow. He left a book beside her bed, a new bestseller called *Getting over Adultery*. On the back there was a photograph of the authors, a handsome Dr. Lou Grossman, who had, the back jacket blurb cheerfully informed even the most cursory reader in bold letters, CHEATED ON HIS WIFE, Helen, pictured beside him, and lived not only to tell the tale but—quite clearly—to get rich off his repentance. They looked so pert, so polished, so intact. She read one page of their uplifting take on infidelity—how it could actually "strengthen a marriage"—and threw it away.

"Don't bring any more books," she said to her husband.

He left her alone after that. The notes dwindled. The circles under his eyes, which had lightened, deepened again. She wondered if he was thinking now, a lot, about the girl. Was she testing him to see if he was really staying? She honestly didn't know. Maybe. She thought: if a man uses pornography and then makes love to you, you figure he's seeing other bodies, body parts—mouths and breasts and splayed-out crotches overlaid on your mouth and breast and crotch. A few of Caroline's friends had complained about their husbands using pornography and how it made them feel. But if it's been about love, then what he sees instead of you is a whole someone else, a face over-laid on your face. Caroline kept seeing that face in his face and wondered when she would get over it. And how.

She decided to take a trip. She figured if she could take a trip and get unsnagged from the fear, not worry about what William was or was not doing, that would help. She would begin to feel safe again somehow. That was the conscious thinking. Underneath it was something else: the idea that a flirtation of her own might somehow awaken her limbs, rid them of the dread that weighed them down. She would certainly not want him to find out. It would be her secret. It would put them back on an even keel. That was the clumsy, semi-conscious thinking. So on a retreat weekend with four of her foundation colleagues—which she normally would have avoided—she allowed herself to go to bed with a younger man who had been flirting with her and insinuating that he would be only too happy to have an affair. A perfectly nice-looking young man, tall with crinkly blue eyes and a receding hairline. Clearly not a sociopath. He liked the kids and they liked him. Who better to vet a prospective lover than a child?

"Is this the weekend?" he'd said to her the previous Thursday, a whispering smile as he leaned over her desk, kid noises in the background.

"Don't count on it," she'd responded. But she was smiling and her "no" was different than usual and she saw that he saw that. She had set things in motion. The day before she went away, she was anxious. She looked at her body in the mirror—glancingly. Good enough, she figured, and they would surely keep the lights off, wouldn't they? For years only William had seen it, William, whom she could now, instead of hate, feel tenderness toward in the name of what she was about to do to him. Poor William. How delicious it was to pity him. She was feeling better already.

Oh my, how wrong could you get it? So wrong you could actually laugh—as she did—the morning she awoke, cold and embarrassed, in some quaint little bed and breakfast in Carmel Valley. The canopied bed was empty. There were doilies everywhere, pinned to the armrests of the velvet settee, atop the chest of drawers. A gagging amount of quaintness. She hadn't even noticed before—not really—so intent was she on getting laid. That was the phrase. She had never used it before, not about anybody. It had always struck her as particularly crude, more so than some of the X-rated expressions. And, as she might have expected had she thought it through at all, she was terrible at it: at getting laid. Way back when, losing her virginity and then the second time—there was deliberation on her part, an intent to get laid, and the sex had been lousy both times. But since William, with him, there had been nothing like that. Sure, there had been times of discrepant lust, times when Caroline felt as if she were servicing him, or, occasionally, he her, times when one or the other just wanted to have sex, no tenderizing embroidery. But that was wholly different. This, here, in this fussy, doily-ridden B&B, was something else, something without even lust, certainly on her part. Not that he wanted that, this man. Not at all. Winkingly, he'd suggested a fling. But it was clear now, lying next to his slender, firm body ("150 sit-ups a day," he said pridefully, when she ran her palm against his taut tummy, he mistaking her appraisal as approval rather than what it was—the stroking of an absence), that he wanted more: engagement, tenderness, connectedness. He tried, he worked over her, he nibbled, he stroked, he smiled. He wasn't here just to get laid and that thought as he caressed her left breast with his lips, the one where she'd had the biopsy, made her even more frantic to get it over with. She reached for his penis, but he gently removed her hand.

"Slow down," he said, "we have all night." And: "I've been waiting a long time for you."

She tried but had no experience with it, with just lying back, purring if need be—the ego-preserving fakery women talked about. She had never had to fake an orgasm and realized, in that moment, how truly incubated she had been by her marriage. Not that she had one every time. But she didn't have to go pretending either. She felt him begin to sense her disinterest, her deep, repelled disinterest and sensed a tightening in him, an incipient anger, and for a moment she actually had a flash of fear. She tried harder, pushing his head down, trying to pass off her urgency as hunger, but he was on to her now and was suddenly sitting bolt upright next to her.

"What's going on?" he asked, reaching to switch on the light. She shielded her eyes with the back of her arm and withdrew into a corner of the four-poster bed.

"I'm sorry," she said, continuing to avoid his eyes.

"Screw you," he said sharply. "I don't like being used."

"I didn't think you'd mind," she said as coquettishly as she could.

"Go to hell," he said. "You fucking women are all alike. You whine about being used and then turn around and use anyone you want. It's pathetic. You're pathetic. Go home where you belong."

She thought for a moment that he could hit her and in her nervousness emitted a kind of strangled giggle. He glared at her and she stopped instantly. She realized she knew nothing about this man, not really. Sure, they'd been colleagues for a stretch of months and, yes, done a little flirting, but that's all. She had no idea what, if any, complicated coils were within him.

"I really am sorry," she said, "I'm over my head here."

But he wasn't interested in any apologies.

"Run home to your hubby where you belong—if he's still there," he said.

"What's that supposed to mean?" she said.

"Don't pull this little-girl shit," he said. "You know damn well what I mean. You're obviously trying to get back at him for something, probably having an affair himself."

She flushed.

"I thought so," he said.

He didn't say another thing. He finished dressing with his back to her and he was gone, slamming the door behind him. Her heart was pounding. She got up and bolted the door and huddled back under the canopy with the light still on. She felt dumb and she felt dirty. She got up and filled the bathtub and lay in it, periodically putting in more hot water. Clearly she had failed adultery 101. Her clumsy attempt at score-settling had put her farther away from where she thought she was going: home, restored. And farther away from the world William had been in. She had been "sport-fucking"—to borrow his phrase, or at least trying to. He had been in love. She felt more keenly the distance between them while recognizing the simple truth: she was an anachronism, a one-man woman, completely that. And the realization of how thoroughly that was true she had relearned in bed with this virtual stranger and it only made her more vulnerable now, not less, as she had hoped. She wasn't cut out for this extramarital world. She wasn't a good game player. She had no idea what the rules were, how to behave, how not to hurt and get hurt. She'd told him the truth: she was over her head here. Thinking about the fury and hurt in his face, she had a residual flash of fear. Not that he really would have struck her. Or that he would tell. But there was some lurking apprehension that kept her heart pounding.

She finally got out of the bath and got back into bed. There was no TV—that's what you got with all this assaultively cheery Victoriana (made one long for a good, plastic motel). She tried to read, but was unsuccessful and finally fell asleep for a few hotly contested hours. She woke to the empty bed, remembering instantly what had happened—or not happened—and was, yes, able to laugh for a minute, at the prissy romance-novel chamber in which she had attempted her first—and it would turn out, only—extramarital copulation. She limped home down the coast highway, carrying her self-inflicted secret, driving slowly, trying to breathe and feel safe, small waves of nausea and humiliation hitting her now and again. It was March, cool and mostly overcast, the sun making pallid streaks in the clouds over the steel-colored water. She stopped that day at the Los Angeles County Line, at a crummy windswept place on the wrong side of the highway, the non-ocean side, that she and William loved to take the kids to on just such grayish days, bundled up, everybody eating paper plates full of steamed shrimp in a musty glassed-in patio, their hands greasy with the butter they dipped the shrimp in, William licking everybody's fingers in turn—Katie's, Steven's, even hers, when they were done, the kids laughing, all of them laughing. She arrived home exhausted, crawled into another bath—she was still feeling dirty—and into bed and that's where William, coming home at nine from an early dinner with Katie, found her: back in their bed. He said nothing about the bedroom relocation, asked nothing beyond the siblinglike chitchat they had fallen into: How was the trip? You look tired. Meeting good?

If he suspected what she'd been doing, he certainly didn't indicate it. He undressed in the bathroom and came, silently, to bed. She meant to fling herself at him, into him, around him, but held back for fear of being too obvious. She would be careful, move back toward him. He turned on the news. There were marines being buried.

"Here's a great patriotic photo op for the prez," he said. He went on, but she didn't hear the words. He might be able to resist talking to her, but he could never resist talking to the TV. Oh God, she loved him. And she wanted to say it, shout it, sing it, but suddenly it all just backed up in her: the weeks of limbo, the bombardment of memory, the terror at his defection, the embarrassment over her own fumbled indiscretion got all tangled up with the intent to love and forgive—carefully rehearsed on the drive down, gaining determination with every mile—so they lay there, side by side, chatting about Ronald Reagan and his dead marines and Katie and her latest boyfriend, a prissy young guy from the DA's office.

"At least this one's not married," William said with a laugh, before he realized—she could see the flicker in his eye—that he was sailing into dangerous waters.

"So, are we any closer to grandchildren?" she said, quickly covering for him.

"Nope. I'm afraid it's just you and me, kid," he said. Where had that come from—that "kid"? He never called her that. Never. She rolled over and reached to turn off her light. He did the same but kept the news on a while longer and then, the TV still on, fell into a hard, snoring sleep. She leaned to look at him. He looked so himself, so innocent. It was crazy: marriage. You gave your whole life, your whole happiness, over to one other human being, even the best of them inept at times, prone to reach for some other fulfillment, some other pleasure. And if you were married the way she was, right to the nerve endings, you lived, she saw now, in particular peril. That was the joke. Mediocre marriages weren't in jeopardy—not the same way. They rolled along absorbing insults because the expectations were lower. Or they fell apart. But the good ones—they were the ones that got damaged. Long, long after they were re-engaged with each other, taking their trips, sitting in piazzas late into starry Italian nights—William himself again, ebullient and opinionated even in a language he didn't speak, everyone wanting to be around him—making love in small, single beds beneath mosquito netting in some small tropical country, she still sometimes saw the young woman's pretty, unscrubbed face (something could trigger it: William using that awful word, "kid," as in "hey, kid, let's pick up the pace here," as they walked up the side of a mountain somewhere; or a letter from home about someone else whose husband had left her; or the sighting, in one of those piazzas or trattorias, of a handsome gray-haired man and a nubile, coltish girl, looking together—Caroline couldn't deny it—transgenerationally provocative so you couldn't help but imagine them contortedly naked together in some lightly shuttered afternoon hotel room, their bodies slatted by sunlight, she a lithe, lascivious whisper astride his hips), still had moments of fear that she could come back to claim him, that he was hers to reclaim if she wanted him, which kept her, Caroline, just a smidgen from a total recapitulation to her marriage, something she only realized—or only truly articulated to herself—that morning when his head dropped forward and she reached to catch him over the breakfast table, missing, in that instant, all that she, with her stubborn, self-contained pride, had already missed by turning down the volume on her own ardor and, over time, on his, domesticating it, in effect, so it couldn't again wander wild. She never got back in the cave with him. Turns out she was a pro, after all, a game player to game play with the best of them. If he knew it, he never said. He let her be. But she knew it in that moment of terror, reaching for him and holding him in those endless minutes 'til the paramedics came, so that in the hospital after she was not only trying to learn how to be without him but also how to accommodate the knowledge of the almost imperceptible yet determined daily squandering of love of which she herself had been the architect. Which is why she was so sure that, in an act of poetic justice, the younger woman would come pay a last visit: to see what Caroline had done. She was the only one who would know it, who would smell it in an instant. Oh baby baby baby, Caroline said, holding his heavy, silent head in those minutes on the floor, waiting, waiting, waiting for the paramedics to come. Don't leave me. Please don't leave me.

The phone rang, startling her, but she didn't get out of bed to get it. She felt guilty for a moment; surely it was Katie. But she didn't have

the energy for her now, knowing she'd pay a price in the morning—
which she did.

"Where were you last night?" her indignant daughter asked when
she reached her at seven the next morning. "I was frantic."

"Probably just in the bathroom or down the hall."

"How's Wills?"

"He's the same, sweetheart. Listen, we need to do something."

"Can't it wait? I've got a lot on my plate in the next couple of
days."

"No, Katie," Caroline said sharply, piercing her daughter's coping
mechanism. "We've waited long enough. Nothing's going to change
now. You need to come. It's time."

"I'll see what I can do."

"Do that."

"Tell Steven to call me."

Brother and sister were there, arms around each other, for the
untethering. Not that any of them were in the room, even Caroline.
They were not. The nurses shooed them into the hall while the doctors disengaged him from all the life-sustaining machinery and
pulled the breathing tube up out of his chest. It took about fifteen
minutes, the three of them standing in the hall, mother and son
standing quietly, Katie fidgeting, walking up and down with her cell
phone to her ear. Reentering the room was reentering a different,
teasing reality—teasing because William, without all the tubes,
looked so well, so intact. He was breathing with sweet, easy regularity still. His cheeks were pink, his body still robust. He was not mea-
ger through cancer nor pinched through pain. He had not wasted
away. The man they looked down on could easily, it seemed, have
walked out the door on his own two legs. Nobody said much. They
came and went, each of them, singly and in pairs and occasionally as
a trio, everybody saying very little. Steven tried to get Katie or Caro-

line to go eat something with him, but neither woman was up to that.

"Jesus, Steven," Katie said, "even at a time like this, you think about food." But she said it with irritable love.

The nurse came, a slender, young one with a narrow face. She said she was going to give him a sedative just so he didn't struggle, even from the depths. Katie left at that moment and didn't come back for forty-five minutes. Caroline stayed. The room was now pretty bare. Steven had set about dismantling it the Tuesday afternoon after their Monday-evening decision. He figured it was better for his mother not to have to do it afterward. The flowers were gone, the stacks of newspapers recycled, and Caroline's clothes and makeup bag were already packed and sitting by the door. The set was all but struck. They would make a clean, quick getaway. Caroline watched the heart monitor, its peaks and valleys. Finally the peaks and valleys got irregular, slower. Katie came back. She and Steven put their hands on their father, the warmth, just as they'd been told, now concentrated in his chest and face. His limbs, fingers, toes, knees, ankles, thighs were already cold. His small nipples, visible now because they'd turned the sheet back to chase the waning warmth of his body (Caroline hearing their summertime kid-shouts in some lake, Tahoe, Arrowhead, Isabella: "Stevie, Stevie, come over here quick, I've found a warm spot. You won't believe it." Steven, treading water, hollering back: "No, no, come here, mine's better.") still looked, to her, so jaunty and adolescent. A part of the body that didn't seem to age: nipples. She watched her children, holding so tightly to each other, blotting the periodic tears from each other's faces. She watched them watching her. It seemed so surreally slow, as if it were taking hours and days and years, but, in fact, within just three hours and twenty minutes of his disconnection, the heart monitor went flat—just like in the movies, a low, flat line. The nurse was immediately there. Katie had her head down on her father's cool belly, issuing forth a low, sustained sob.

"It's not fair," she kept saying, "it's not fair."

Caroline, still intact, held Steven close. That, too, seemed to stretch forever, that moment of maximum, immediate loss, as if they were suspended there, the three of them, in some artist's rendering of captured grief. Then Caroline forcibly gathered up her strong, smart, savvy daughter from her father's body, tucked her hard against her breast, and, with Steven behind carrying the two small suitcases, they left the room and went down the elevator and out into the bright, sunny William-less afternoon.

They slept together, the three of them, in Caroline and William's bed, Katie's ragged sorrow finally quieted with a couple of stiff drinks and an Ativan. They tucked her in and she slept. Mother and son lay fully clothed side by side, watching some old movie, holding hands. They'd talked briefly about services and speeches and all the funeral folderol, while in truth, they simply wanted to hole up here together, shut the doors, and have his still-vivid presence all to themselves. The much vaunted intact nuclear family was probably not, Caroline thought, as she wandered the halls and the house after she had awakened and slipped out of bed leaving her two grown, sleeping children, the most sensible unit if you wanted some emotional bench strength. But they had lived so thoroughly and instinctively in it, the four of them, that everybody else had always been secondary. No wonder the kids hadn't married. They were still babies sleeping in their parents' bed. Parent's bed. She didn't need to shoulder all the responsibility. There were other reasons. They came from a generation, an educated, eternally young slice of it anyway, that married late, if at all. It could still happen. Steven might yet marry and produce the next Betts. But it was not a bet, on this night of loss, that Caroline would put any money on. This was it then: them. She would have to do her best to try to shoo them away some, just as the nurse—with her adamant kindness—had shooed them into the hall earlier in the day.

Restless, Caroline kept wandering. She actually thought about driving down to the ocean and watching the sun come up, but knew the kids would be alarmed if one or the other came to and found her missing. So she paced, finally pouring herself a tumbler of cognac and lying down on the old, cracked leather sofa in William's study. Finally she tiptoed back into the bedroom and found the Ativan bottle and took one herself. There were things to be gotten through. It took another half hour, another half snifter of brandy, and she drifted into a daze more than a sleep right there on the sofa, waking hours later to the sound of laughter—Katie's big roar—and the smell of something Steven was clearly at work on. It was noon. In the kitchen, her red-eyed kids were concertedly lifeful. Both had aprons on and Steven, arms around his sister from behind, was trying to teach her the proper way to chop an onion.

"She's hopeless, Mom, absolutely hopeless. No one will ever marry her."

"Someone already did, smarty."

"Yeah well . . ."

"Yeah well, what? I left him. He didn't leave me. And he certainly didn't expect me to cook."

"Thank God. Or the marriage'd have been shorter than it was."

"Screw you."

"Mom, have you noticed, she swears when I get her."

"Mom, we turned off the phone so you'd be able to sleep. Your phone service probably has a zillion messages."

"Right," Caroline said. "Let's eat first and we'll face the hordes afterward. I'll just go up and splash some water on my face and be right back." As she turned to leave, she saw that Steven's arms had tightened around his sister, his head was in her neck, and both now were crying again.

They ate Mexican eggs, or Steven did while his sister and mother pushed theirs around, struggling to get a bite or two down. Caroline had plugged the phone back in and it started to ring continuously, but none of them made a move to answer it. There were no other immediate family members to bring into the loop or into the house—no spouses or children or sisters. A nuclear knot.

"Katie, we'll need to get something to the newspapers. Can you manage that?"

"Yeah. OK."

They disbanded to their chores, Katie to her father's office, Steven back to the kitchen to clean up, and Caroline upstairs to tackle the messages. It was a blur of obligations. Periodically she'd hear her grown children downstairs laughing or squabbling, as they'd always done, and then long stretches of silence, when, she figured, they were simply holding on to each other. By the end of the day, the plans were set: the obituary, the funeral, the menu—which Steven had labored over, open cookbooks spread everywhere on the dining-room table. They sipped large, potent margaritas—Steven had made a market run—and ate guacamole and chips for dinner then piled again together into the big bed. Somewhere in the middle of the night, Steven crawled off to his own room. But Katie, sleeping in one of her father's T-shirts, stayed. Caroline kept a hand on her back as she slept, stroking her when she got squirmy and restless. Her baby. She herself didn't want to take any more sleeping pills if she could help it, because they always left her residually foggy, and there was going to be a lot to do. She finally drifted off herself, waking to Katie's trying-to-be-quiet sobs. She scooped her close again, saying nothing, and both, through blurry eyes, watched the dawn come through the magnolia tree. They must have slept again because both awoke some hours later to the telltale signs of Steven once again at his culinary post—the faraway banging of pots and some rich smell wafting up the stairs.

"He's a maniac," Katie said, laughing.

"He's going to feed us in spite of ourselves."

"What do you think it is, this time?"

"I don't know. Smells pretty exotic."

"Mom," Katie said finally, "do you think I have to speak at the funeral?"

"It's up to you, sweetheart."

"Don't you think people will expect it?"

"Yeah, I suppose, but I still think it's up to you. You've got a couple of days to think about it."

"You're not going to say anything, are you?"

"No. You know I'm not very good at that stuff. I'll leave it to the rest of you."

"Do you think Steven wants to?"

"What do you think?"

"I think he probably just wants to cook for everybody instead."

"Who else, though? Have you guys talked about it? Is there somebody else we should ask?"

"Martin, certainly, and that guy who worked with him on the prisoners' rights campaign. Be nice to try to find one of those Vietnam guys he counseled."

"That's a long way back."

"I know, but that was a good time for him."

"Any of your friends?"

"What, to speak?"

"That. Or just to make sure they're invited. Some of the ones that were around all those years."

"Maybe I'll ask Linda. She always says he helped her get through law school and then convinced her not to practice. She's funny and we can use some of that."

"What about that other young woman that you were so close to for a minute right after law school?"

"Cammie?"

"No, the dark-haired one from San Francisco. You guys were inseparable for a while."

"Oh yeah, April. Is that the one you mean?"

There was the name spoken out loud in the house after fifteen years. "Yes," her mother said evenly. "That one."

"She died," Katie said.

"Died?" Caroline finally managed to say. "When?" She was looking hard out the window so Katie couldn't see her face.

"Years ago," Katie said. "Didn't you know? It was awful."

Caroline's fist was against her mouth. Katie went on. "One of those big pileups on I-5. It was that next summer after she was around. No, it must have been the fall because that's when it gets all foggy in the middle there. Something like six people died."

Six people. I-5. Years ago. Caroline, biting a knuckle to keep from moaning, moaned anyway, a big, open-wounded moan. Years dead. Years and years and years. Only Caroline had kept her alive. She was a witch, a sorceress, a conjurer, a fool: she had, single-mindedly, kept someone alive—the totemic siren standing at the foot of her marriage bed, and later, beside the hospital bed where he had died.

"Mom," Katie said, leaning up to look at her, "you OK?"

"Mmm," Caroline said, trying to steady her breathing, mumbling something about loss.

"I thought you knew."

Caroline got up quickly, heading to the bathroom, Katie shouting after her. "You know what's funny. She didn't want to practice law either. She'd moved back to San Francisco and was working in a publishing house. Can you imagine—after all that studying we did?"

Caroline heard Katie give a sharp little laugh. Out there somewhere in a different room, in a different world, on a different planet, her daughter was laughing, while she, clutching the side of the sink, stared at herself in the mirror: a brunette with gray roots showing, her face a twisted mask of sorrow-filled jocularity. Is that me? That's me. The joke's on me. Oh baby, baby, baby.

"Mom," Katie yelled in, "I'm going to go shower. I'll see you downstairs."

At the funeral, Steven and Katie got the giggles. Caroline looked sharply at them but it was no good. One had started, then the other. They stepped back from the grave site—that's where it happened—and tried to become invisible in the crowd, but their tittering followed them. They were still holding hands and later, when Caroline asked them in the limousine on the way back to the house what had been so funny, they showed her the fingernail marks they'd made in their arms to try to stem the laughter.

"We really tried," they said, setting off again.

"What was so funny?" she said.

"Did you see Martin's head?" Steven said. "Those new plugs . . ."

"These little rows of hair," Katie interrupted, and they were off again. Caroline knew it was their antidote to grief so she left them alone. It was done anyway. All done, save the feasting. Steven had been cooking nonstop for forty-eight hours—pâtés and quiches and beautiful little tarts. Caroline moved through the reception—is that what it was called? Did one have a reception after a funeral? It sounded so formal, so jolly—as she had moved in and around her children in the last couple of days: strong, warm, seemingly present, gracefully accepting compliments (on her children; on her hair; oh yes, she'd say, reaching up to touch it, I'd forgotten) and condolences. Nobody seemed to notice that she wasn't there. After about an hour, Katie asked everyone to gather in the living room and invited people to speak. Martin, as his oldest friend, would go first. Katie had warned Steven to hide in the kitchen when he heard her call people into the living room. Even then she had to do it, clutch her forearm with fingernails to keep from losing it again, knowing Steven was in there no doubt doubled over. She heard some of what Martin said, but it came through the scrim of her suppressed laughter. A couple of other people got up, then Linda and she did tell the story about Mr. Betts, as she still called him, urging her to go to law school and then telling her not to practice, to do something more worthwhile. The many lawyers present laughed. Katie spoke last, looking well over everyone's heads. No eye contact. Steven was beside her. She said it was lousy to be in your forties and never have lost anybody because you had no practice at all at it, not that anyone had practice losing a father. Doubly lousy, it was, she said, if your father was funny and fair and a feminist before anyone was even using the word. She said: "I know some of you out there are the suppliers of the really bad jokes my father forwarded on to me. So now that he's not here, I'm going to give you my E-mail address so you can just send them . . ." and then she did lose it, tears cascading freely, and Steven stepped in and said: "On behalf of my mother and sister, I want to thank you all for coming. Please eat and drink and talk. My father . . . would have wanted that."

"Can I just say something?" It was the Bettses' lifetime friend Maggie, a heavyset woman with a blonde shag and piercing blue eyes. She began talking as she moved toward the front of the room. "I just want to toast—I don't know if that's appropriate or not under the circumstances—but I want to toast Caroline and William. Their marriage was a source of inspiration to the rest of us. To you," she said, turning toward Caroline and raising her glass, "and your marriage. I just want you to know," she said with a laugh, "we were all jealous as hell."

People lingered. A couple of them—not close friends—actually asked Steven for some recipes. "It's tacky, but you can't blame them," his sister said when everyone had finally gone and the three of them were alone in William's office eating off paper plates. "It's a good new specialty for you," she said to her brother. "Gourmet funerals. No, no, I've got it: Funereal Feasts. How 'bout that? Cortege crudités. Graveyard gravlax. Or maybe: Mourning Meals."

"All right, you don't need to pound it to death," Steven said.

"I really do think it's a good idea."

"Yeah, yeah. Hey, Mom, did you get a good look at Martin's plugs?" Steven said, beginning to sputter again.

"You'd think," Katie said, "in this town, you could get a better job. Jesus—we're in cosmetics central here."

Caroline smiled at them.

"Mom, you OK?"

"Fine."

"Here let me refill you," Steven said getting up. "You didn't try the veal loaf."

"How'd you think Linda looked?" Katie said.

"Older, but nice," Caroline said. "She always did look old-fashioned—those floaty dresses."

"Yeah, I agree. I think it looks good on her, though I can't imagine wearing any of that stuff."

"What'd I miss?" Steven asked bouncing back onto the sofa.

"Linda," Katie said.

"She looked good."

"I didn't say she didn't."

"She's not my type, but there's something sort of comforting about her."

"What is your type? This entire family has been trying to figure that out for years."

"You should talk."

"Oh come on, lighten up."

"I hate that expression. People always use it when they've insulted you and you don't think it's funny."

"I don't like it either," Caroline said softly.

" 'Atta girl, Mom," Steven said.

"She always takes your side," Katie said.

"You guys," Caroline said.

"I know who's my type," Steven said. "That Cammie. She looks great."

"I think she's had a boob job."

"You're just jealous."

"Screw you."

"I rest my case."

"She's about to marry that guy that was with her. He seemed nice enough. You know she has a daughter who's starting college. Can you believe it?"

"You could have had one that age if you and Jamie had done it," Steven said.

"We did do it."

"You know what I mean."

"Screw you."

"You just said that."

"I'm saying it again." There was no heat in the exchange. It was just elbowing sibling banter, comforting in its familiarity. Caroline took no notice.

"Mom, you know I asked Cammie if she remembered about April. She actually went to the funeral. It was in some small chapel in the city where you could see the water. She remembered seeing Daddy there. I'd forgotten he'd gone. I guess I'd told him about the accident. He must have been up there for something."

Caroline made some strange, animal-like noise. What had she been thinking? Of course he would go. Of course he would be there. She could see him sitting in a pew: his overcoat, his big square head, his red-rimmed eyes, the bay out the window shimmering under a lifting blanket of sun-flecked fog. Of course he was there. He was a man in love. A man in mourning. Her husband. The man she now mourned. A momentary pang of the old, sharp anger leavened her grief. How sweet and pure it was—the hate. How nice to hate him again and not herself. But it all got blurry again very fast: the love, the hate, the loss.

It wasn't going to stay nailed down. Even with him dead. With the girl dead. Dead, dead, dead, dead, dead. That was the real joke. They were both dead now. Yet, sorceress that she was, she had kept the girl alive and now she would keep him alive. She could do it. She'd had years of practice. And if that meant that some days, he was going to be sitting in the pew, hunched up with sorrow, so be it. On other days, he would be with her, Caroline, in that automobile, when everything was new and he smelled like heaven. Or earth. More that than heaven. Oh, she would go through the motions of a normal, present-tense life. People expected that. They needed it for their own reasons. She would oblige, she would pretend to be fine, to be getting on with it or else someone— one of her kids or well-meaning friends—would try to haul her off to some so-called grief counselor or widow's group. But she was skillful. She would get around them all. Hadn't she done it before?

"Mom." Katie said it like it was a three-syllable word. "You all right?"

"I'm finally just letting down," Caroline said.

"You're entitled," said her daughter, eagerly reassured.

"Who are we talking about anyway?" Steven said.

"My friend April. Remember. She was that really tall, pretty girl I studied for the bar with."

"Vaguely," Steven said.

"You remember, we studied for the bar together all that summer. And—I told Mom—she was just like Linda. She didn't want to practice law either. I'm the only asshole apparently that was gung-ho for the new drill. Big-time career, no kids—the whole nine yards."

"You're not an asshole," Steven said softly, and he reached for her as she started to cry again.

"I want my daddy," she said, as Steven held her and rocked her.

They all ended up in their separate bedrooms. They huddled for a little while in Caroline's room, then drifted off to their own. She was, for the first time, alone in the bed. She couldn't stand it. She got up and dressed and tiptoed out of the house in her walking clothes, shoes squishing on the wooden floors. It was cold and dark, but the streetlights were on and she had that old familiar immunity from fear that sorrow conferred. Like somebody in a small town, she could walk through her whole life. It was all right there in a half-mile radius, the little town with its video shops and tacky pizza parlors, the hospital, even the fraternity house—pretty dilapidated by now, its Greek letters askew. She started to do it, make the memorial loop, but realized it was too soon. Way, way too soon, she said half out loud, hugging her arms around her. She turned around and went home. It was misty and cool and the newspapers hadn't come yet. They usually got there around four. Sometimes she and William would get home at one or two, if they'd been downtown to a concert and then had dinner somewhere on the eastside, and William would make coffee so he could stay awake for the telltale thud in the driveway or on the lawn.

"I can't wait 'til morning to read them," he'd say excitedly. "You go ahead to bed."

She would go on up and undress and get into bed and doze off waiting for him, semi-asleep until he was there beside her.

A MARRIED MAN

"I THINK WE SHOULD go see the guy," Marcia said. The kids were at a sleepover with their grandparents.

"What guy?" her husband said.

"You know perfectly well who I'm talking about."

"I do?"

"Oh come on, David. If you want to keep doing it this way, feel free. But it isn't working."

"It's not? I thought we were doing fine under the circumstances. Nobody's thrown anything or screamed in front of the children. I did have that one bad moment in the beginning, but hey, that's to be expected. Since then, I think we've been doing great."

"You do? Is this what you think a marriage should be?"

"Is this what I think a marriage should be?"

"You're going to keep doing it, aren't you?"

"Doing what?"

"You know perfectly well what."

"What would you have me do? I think I'm holding up remarkably well."

"Are you saying you won't go see him?"

"I don't know."

"Well, who should we ask?"

"Why don't we ask you. You have all the answers. Is David here going to go see Mr. New Beginnings? It'd have been easier if you'd found something with a different name. This one's particularly cloying, don't you think? I mean, even you think that, right? You haven't lost all your sense of judgment."

She ignored the last remark. "Yeah, I know it sounds corny, but Marlene said . . ."

"Marlene. Oh they've been in this boat, too? Do you all talk about this stuff?"

"I'm not telling anyone what happened. I just asked her for the name of a therapist. It's not like everyone we know hasn't done it."

"Screwed around?"

"Counseling. No one stays married anymore without some help."

"They don't. It seems to me we were doing just fine."

"Obviously there were some unresolved issues."

"Unresolved issues, huh? Then we need an arms negotiator instead of a therapist."

"Have it your way. I'm going to make an appointment and go see him whether you want to or not. I'll leave you an E-mail tomorrow and tell you when and where and you can show up or not."

"Isn't E-mail great, the perfect medium for an intimate communiqué. 'See you at New Beginnings on blankety blank day at blankety blank hour. Your loving wife.' Just makes you warm all over."

David had taken to talking like this ever since it happened. He heard himself sounding like an actor in a B-grade sitcom—one little jousting bon mot after the other—but he couldn't seem to help it. Was this where the modern married man went when injured? You couldn't flail or knock anybody out, certainly not a woman. You couldn't stand in the middle of the room and say, "You what, you fucking cunt?" when that's exactly what you wanted to say, because evolved men of your station did not, under any circumstances, use the "C" word about or toward their wives—not even in the locker room, not even to themselves, truth be told. Not nice men like David Sanderson and his pals. On the other hand, you weren't supposed to do the other either: just melt there in sobs on the living-room floor like some pathetic defeated dog, because that wasn't cool either.

"We wanted you guys to feel things," Karen, the wife of his friend Marty, said when telling a story about how her husband was so overcome with emotion in the delivery room he couldn't hold his hand steady to cut the umbilical cord, "but there are limits."

She said it with a certain tender smile, but every man there, the two other husbands—at their regular Friday-night gathering—got the message. There was a fine line of new-male decorum and it went slicing right down the middle between macho and wimp and most of the time, by nature and upbringing, David Sanderson and his friends prided their evolved selves on being able to walk it, no sweat. But when something happened, something bad, something awful and unnerving and dislocating—as had certainly happened to David—there wasn't much wiggle room in there so, by default, he had fallen into this fakely cheerful, sitcomish badinage as a way of putting a Band-Aid on both: his towering macho rage and his wimpy pathetic shattered heart.

"I didn't mean to do it," Marcia said.

David was looking at her. She was not looking at him but rather at Mr. New Beginnings, a burly, gray-haired man in some sort of soft, expensive-looking, multicolored sweater who looked more like a nattily dressed construction boss on a night out than a repentant adulterer (though, come to think of it, what did they look like?). That was his claim to fame. He'd done it himself and had made a fortune telling America how his marriage survived and how theirs could, too. David

had been hoping that he would look and sound repellently caring, full
of that smarmy telegenic wisdom much in vogue in recent years
because he figured then they would be out of here. Even Marcia
wouldn't sit still for that, would she? They'd laughed at such people,
watched them sometimes on PBS—these psycho-sexual healers were
the mainstay now of pledge drives—then imitated them, their
bathetic bromides about recovery and forgiveness. Marcia herself, just
last year—or was it the year before?—had given David for his birthday a bumper sticker that said: MY INNER CHILD WAS STILLBORN. He
hadn't put it on his car, but they'd certainly had a good laugh over it
and it was still stuck up somewhere in his home office. Where was it
though—over the fax or above the copy machine? Sitting here watching his pretty, dark-haired wife, in profile so that he was looking right
at her diamond studs—the square ones he'd bought her when their
second baby, Kyle, was born about six weeks premature, so he had to
stay in the hospital and they went every day to visit him, holding
hands, and one day David, on a whim, drove right straight from the
hospital, because they'd just gotten the news that Kyle was going to be
fine and could come home in another couple of days, to Tiffany's in
Beverly Hills and took her right in and bought the earrings—David
couldn't exactly remember where the bumper sticker was. Was it
above the fax? He heard Mr. NB talking quietly to his wife and saw
the light flashing off the studs as her jaw moved to answer and he figured maybe he could just stay like this—slightly invisible—and the
whole thing would go away. Maybe it hadn't happened at all. Maybe
this was all some ghastly hysterical dream. This couldn't be them—
David and Marcia Sanderson—sitting here in this homey beige office
in the Valley with its catchy needlepoint pillows (I'M OK; YOU'RE SICK
and TO ERR IS HUMAN; TO SEEK THERAPY DIVINE) getting ready to spill
their conjugal guts to this avuncular-looking former philanderer with
a clearly telegraphed—yuk, yuk—sense of embroidered humor. Cannot be. It simply cannot be.

"Mr. Sanderson?"

"What?"

"Did you hear what your wife said?"

"Only vaguely. I was really wondering how you came up with 'New Beginnings'?"

"Here he goes," Marcia said. "That's all he's been doing since . . ."

"Since what?" David said. He was now not facing his wife but looking instead at his—say it ain't so—adulterous adultery counselor. "Since you . . ." He didn't know what to say, what to call it, so he stopped. "I just wanted to make a literary point here before we get to the juicy stuff: I mean, doctor, have you ever heard of old beginnings?"

The man smiled, not his full wattage klieg-light smile, just a little tweaky one. "You've got a point there," he said. (Obviously somebody had leeched every iota of defensiveness out of him; maybe that's what happened when you confessed to straying and got cleansed.) "It is sort of corny. Helen came up with it. It grew on me though."

Clearly Helen was the wronged wife. David could see her picture on the nearby bookshelf. He remembered seeing a picture of her somewhere else. Had Marcia shown him one on the back of some book? He couldn't quite remember. That was one thing for sure: since his wife's escapade—that was the best he could do at the moment, "escapade"; it had a kind of festival air, like the pillows—his memory had been blurry at best. That's why he, of the ferociously retentive brain (columns of numbers he could remember with dead accuracy, clients' holdings, cards in a poker game) could not remember where that damn bumper sticker was—nor where he had seen Helen before. Was it on the tube? After all she and her husband were the Fric and Frac of forgiveness, working the Getting Over Adultery circuit together. They were the ultimate marriage revivalists. He couldn't see the photograph very clearly from where he was sitting, but he remembered this Helen looking pretty great for a woman of her age—what, sixty, sixty-five? No doubt she'd had face work and dyed her hair, and had also, like her husband, probably been denuded of defensiveness, anger, hurt, sorrow, etc., as well as wrinkles. Come to think of it, if he looked closely at Fric, as he did now, he figured him, too, for a little face work—an eye job at the very least. David had never been very good at spotting the surgical repairs that were now seemingly ubiquitous on their side of town (and, yes, even among some of their friends) 'til Marcia had given him a quick, intensive course one day when they'd had a romantic lunch a deux at the little Italian restaurant near their house.

"See, look," she said, gesturing with her head: "that one's had the whole thing, look how the eyes are pulled up, that one probably just a peel. You can see the skin's so white and there are none of those little tiny wrinkles."

And now David, too, looked closely—even at the men. No question, Mr. NB had tweaked a little. Is this where he and Marcia were heading, into this strangely cleansed coupledom, their matching facelifts a testament to their resilience, their New Beginnings?

Lou—as he insisted they call him in his modulated voice—made a corrective. Time to turn away from the hurting husband (not going to make any headway there) and get back to the wife. "So Marcia, what do you think, do you think it matters to him that you didn't mean to do it?" Excellent move, David wanted to say. It was on the tip of his tongue, but he caught himself. He was curious about what his wife would say.

The men looked at her. She looked down. There was a restful if awkward silence. Ball in your court, dear, he wanted to say, but again was able to restrain himself. This, he thought, was progress. She looked up: "I don't know," she said.

"That's not fair," David blurted. "You're not allowed not to know."

He'd blown it and he knew it.

"You can't tell me what to know and not know," Marcia said. "That's his job," she said, gesturing at their cool, calm therapist.

"In fact, it's not," he said. "You two have to figure that out. I'm just here to be your facilitator."

Was there a word more loathsome? Interface, maybe. That luckily had faded out somewhat. But facilitator hung on. David hated it. The other word he hated was proactive. Isn't that, he'd said, at a recent meeting, to one of the aggressive junior partners in his money management firm, a redundancy, a tautology? "Do you really think we have to be proactive?" he'd said, fairly spitting out the "pro" part. "Isn't active active enough without the pro affixed to it?" The rebuked junior didn't have the good grace to be offended. Instead, he flashed a wee conspiratorial smile around the room (as in, "Poor David—he's a little unhinged these days"). Or did he, in fact, flash a smile? Was that just paranoia? It was the memory of that wee, wheedling smile—not anything that Marcia had said or done—that had finally driven David here to see Mr. New Beginnings. Something had to give. He was becoming an object of public pity.

"Are you," he said now to the therapist, "a really proactive facilitator or someone content to sit back and let us try to do the lion's share of interfacing ourselves?"

"You see, he's doing it again," Marcia said. "If he's just going to keep doing that, I suppose there's no point . . ."

"Well, Mrs. Sanderson—Marcia," Lou said. "That's to be expected—a little acting out one way or the other. You must remember that you've already done a little acting out yourself."

At that, David could not restrain himself. In the time-honored child's gesture, he turned to his slightly abashed looking wife, stuck his thumbs in his ears and, waggling his fingers at her, said, "Na-na-na-na-na." Then he fell into giggles.

"This," he said, "is a lot more fun than I thought it was going to be." But by the time he'd finished the sentence, his giggles had devolved into a big gulping grief, which he could not, try as he might, effectively stem. Through his ensuing blur of tears, he saw the therapist raise a cautionary hand to Marcia, stilling her—had to admit the bastard was good—leaving David to blubber on unaccosted. He tucked his face down against his chest. Nobody said anything. In the cavernous silence, his sorrow grew to encompass not just what Marcia had done to him but each and every slight along the male way: not making the basketball team in junior high, his best friend taking the girl he had a crush on to the prom, his terror of losing Kyle right there in the preemie ward before he'd even had a chance to hold him, smell him, all the way back to his own first stitches (just over his left eye where he still had a scar Marcia had routinely kissed, postcoitally, when they were first going together) when his father had said, "Come on Davie, it's not that bad; act like a man." (I was only six!) Was he talking out loud? He didn't think so, but he looked up for a minute to make sure and then dropped his gaze again and recapitulated to the string of sorrows that now seemed inescapably to be of a piece, the very forerunners of his wife's treachery. He tried to wrestle his tears to a draw, conjured up all the heroes of yore—on battlefields and athletic fields—who would never have so much as whimpered let alone wept in public (even in private), let alone in a shrink's office, all the men throughout the ages who'd stood tall and kept their manly dignity in the face of terrible wounds and losses. All of them—he'd let all of them down, his entire gender. Here he was—a fortysomething successful guy with two kids—blubbering his guts out when (to add absolute insult to injury) the man his wife had had sex with (come on, David, say it—the man his wife had fucked) was not only someone he, David, had brought home to dinner, but a decorated war hero to boot who actually, in fact, wore boots (alligator or lizard or some such reptilian skin) with his pressed jeans and blue blazer. The humiliations didn't quit and he wasn't sure how he was going to make peace with any of them, including his own immediate meltdown. What did you do? Dry your eyes, kiss your wife, shake hands with your new marriage counselor, and sail back out into the day? Women were good at this: they could come unglued one moment and re-glue themselves the next. But he didn't have any experience with this and he couldn't imagine how to tuck himself—and his damaged pride—back into his aviator sunglasses and his cream-colored Italian suit jacket folded neatly beside him on the sofa arm and his big, black Grand Cherokee—the tribal layers—and thence, into his high-rise Century City corner office to hide his red-rimmed eyes from the commiserative looks of the secretaries (excuse me, assistants, particularly his own razor-sharp assistant, the gifted young Mindy) who (and this, he was sure, was not paranoia) knew absolutely that his wife had cheated on him, could smell it on him underneath all that expensive tribal camouflage.

As if reading his mind, Lou said, "Don't worry, David. Your behavior's quite natural. (Great. So in addition to everything else, he was a cliché as well.) Remember it's one day at a time—or, as we like to say, one session at a time. Adultery is a very painful thing for a marriage but it can also be a . . ."

"New Beginning," David chimed in.

"Right," the doctor said. "Go home, be nice to your kids, have some fun, and I'll see you next Thursday."

"Great," Marcia said, getting up, no worse for the emotional wear and tear. Course, what had she done? She hadn't wept and made a scene. On the street, she was unbearably considerate, denuded herself—seemingly after one session—of any of the defensiveness that had marked her behavior since she'd dropped her bombshell news three weeks earlier. Gone. Just like that. She'd picked up her cues from Mr. NB in a nanosecond. One verbal slap on the wrist, one modest rebuke, and she got it. She went docile, rolled over, and now stood here smiling at her wounded husband with a beatific all-forgiving smile. (Was it he who needed forgiving?) Maybe there was something in the ether of the office, some piped-in, olfactory something or other that tranquilized the miscreant—not the betrayee, but the betrayer—thereby taking all the heat out of the combat and letting everyone just schmooze and sob their way to new marital health. It was weird. He felt as if he'd entered some hyper-emotional twilight zone where everyone else was a therapized zombie. He started, right there on the street, to cry all over again. He stared straight up into a palm tree, its fronds rustling in the late summer sun, and bit down on his lip to keep the tears from escaping from behind his wire-rimmed sunglasses.

"What do you think, sweetheart," she said, reaching out to touch his arm, "should I pick up some sushi? Juana will have already fed the kids."

It was normalcy. Sweet, sweet normalcy, what a man would sell his soul for, what David had been praying for the return of for three long, agonizing weeks: sweet, marital normalcy. They would be friends again; in time, lovers. They would eat sushi. They would be wed forever. The kids would grow up and do wonderfully in school. They would have friends and barbecues and grow old together and, yes, even laugh in later years about her one little detour years earlier when you, you know, had your little escapade with that guy I brought home, that guy with those terrible alligator boots. Ha, ha, they would laugh together, conjuring up images of the smooth-faced, smooth-talking, soft-sweatered doctor who had, with empathetic deftness, put their marriage back together lickety split. It was too dizzying to contemplate, too dazzling, too sweet.

"Screw you," he said to his wife.

"What did you say?" she asked, removing her hand.

"Screw you," he said, turning and walking away, adding, under his breath, those sweet forbidden words, "you fucking cunt."

The thing was: now what? He went back to his office and collapsed on the sofa. Inside him, tears fought with giggles, jouncing around. He kept swallowing to keep everything down. Breathe David, breathe David, breathe David. He had to fight the temptation to call Marcia on her car phone and tell her he was sorry and that, yes, sushi would be great, even though the thought of food—sushi in particular—made him deeply queasy. Why in the world was everyone eating raw fish anyway? Was it some sort of ritualistic act of purification, some slippery act of self-abnegation? The phone rang a few times but was quickly picked up by his assistant. From his corner office on the twentieth floor, he watched the day ebb and the evening begin—wispy scarves of pink and orange spilling around the adjacent high-rises, flashing colorfully in their reflective surfaces. He loved his office at this time of day, loved to watch the slow collision of day and night, natural light fading—he could actually see, if he scrunched far in the corner, a sliver of the ocean, the sun slipping down behind it—fake lights coming on in the buildings and on the streets. Often, after a long intense day of staring at numbers and taking phone calls from irritable and egomaniacal clients wanting to know why he had or hadn't put their money into this or that, he would stand here at the huge bank of windows looking down on the city, so sprawling and centerless, and his heart would swoop down on the roof of the handsome two-story traditional house where his pretty, pretty wife and his two small sons awaited his imminent homecoming. He'd fairly shiver with the anticipation of rejoining them, the baths, the stories, the snuggling—all four of them piled into bed watching some silly TV show. Other men wanted other things: glory, conquests—professional, athletic, sexual. He knew these men. He worked with them. He played with them. He intimated a comradeship with their unconsummated longings, their midlife frustrations. Too little of this, too much of that: an angry wife, a kid with ADD, a dead-end job, no sex, bad sex, boring sex. He didn't want to seem smug or square. But the truth was he did not want for more. He had everything he had ever wanted. Had had. Now he couldn't even bear to stand at the window and look out toward his little haven. In his mind, he saw a big black dot over his house, erasing it. All gone. Was that what happened to the psychos who came unhinged and killed not only their lying wives but their children, too? For a second he understood it—the need to wipe the whole picture out of your mind as if it had never existed. Her, them, happiness. Blamo! You just didn't want anyone lingering around in the corner of your mind reminding you of what you'd lost. It wasn't really about killing the kids. It was about obliterating the picture of the happy family, which, of course, if the juries would only listen, they—the cunts—had already done anyway.

Finally he dozed off. He vaguely heard the phone ring again, but a deep exhaustion finally had him. When he woke, it was dark. The towers around him were lit up. They looked so cheery. Through some of the windows, he saw the cleaning crews at their work: the nightly sanitation ballet, plie, swish, dust, mop. He looked at his watch: 9:15. He'd missed the baths, the stories. Kyle was no doubt already asleep. His all grown-up and now robust little preemie. That was the funny thing: Kyle, at three, was the assertive one. It was six-year-old Trevor who was shy and skittery, sandy-haired and small-boned—his father's son. That's how it was in most families, David had observed. Each parent had a kid—or kids—who favored him or her. Of course, he'd fight for custody of both of them if it came to that. Yes he would. His half of it anyway. Parenthood by shuttle. Half the kids in their school had divorced or screwed-up parents. They'd been the aberration. Now they'd simply joined the human race, fallen back into it from their sweet, suburban pinnacle. What did he expect? What had he expected? That it would all last?

On automatic pilot, he finally got out of the office and into the parking garage and into his big, black Jeep. It was still hot out and all the low-slung minimalls he passed were jammed with traffic, the fast-food restaurants full, people eating or waiting for their take-out orders: pupusas, falafel, teriyaki. Everywhere you looked, the neon food signs beckoned vibrantly. The music was blaring, thumping. The whole city seemed like it was on one big multicultural date—beautiful mixed-race girls in spandex and chunky shoes with beautiful hyper-inflated men. Everyone was so big, so vibrant, so elemental. Out among them, David felt so small and white and insignificant and slightly silly in his big sports utility vehicle (was its heft some kind of equalizer?), an imposter, an interloper, a fool, a relic. He realized he'd become acutely self-conscious in the past couple of weeks, as if every-body and everything were mocking him—even his own big, dumb, outsized car.

When he got home, it was well past ten and everyone was asleep. He took his shoes off and tiptoed upstairs but saw no light under any door. He was tempted to sneak in and kiss his boys, but Trevor had a hard time sleeping and he didn't want to risk waking anyone. He retreated to the den with a large tumbler of neat Scotch—which he normally didn't drink. No hard liquor. Never really had. But this was an exception. Was it ever. He opened the French doors to the big back garden and warm night air, anchored by far-off freeway noise, blew gently in. A good night. A lucky man, shoes off, Scotch in hand, sur-rounded by dozens of family photos propped up on the tasteful blond wood bookshelves. The cuckold in his kingdom. He caught sight of Marcia's large desk calendar and couldn't resist checking it out—something he would never have done before. It would never even have occurred to him. What did he expect to find? A listing of scheduled assignations? The calendar was dense with entries all in her tiny, immaculate hand. Kyle—ped. 3 P.M. Trevor—teach. conf., 10 A.M. (remind D.). Dinner—Al Fresco, Marts. and Gblemns. 7:30. *Vogue* d-line—Lang. Practically every square was full. There were other deadlines for the other magazine pieces she was working on and other dinners and it looked all so tidy and rich there, a life in shorthand, their life, their full, annotated life and gazing at it, he felt the tears come up again and he swallowed them back. Then he noticed that in every Thursday square for the next month, she had written: "Dr. Lou—4 P.M." Had she added that just today when she got home, after he'd manfully cursed her there on the street and strode off? Was she that cool, that efficient? Had to hand it to her. This was the new breed of women. Never before in the history of the world had so many women been so competent at so many things. It was awe-inspiring. They had their careers and their babies. They were gourmet cooks and self-aware lovers. They could tell you exactly where and how to touch them, how much pressure, no, just there, that's it, not so hard, yes, that's perfect . . . They could do the carving and the barbecuing. They went to the gym and gave birth without drugs. They balanced the checkbook and decorated the house and served on the school auction committee. There wasn't anything they couldn't do. Where had they come from? They had sprung fully formed it seemed from the earth itself like some strange new hybrid. And it had happened overnight, in a generation. He thought of his own mother. She was from a whole different species of women, from a whole other planet, the planet of the aprons, of the perennially overcooked pork chops, of the intractable postpartum pounds, of the public—and no doubt pri-vate—prudery. He couldn't imagine her issuing explicit sexual instructions to anyone anywhere at any time—certainly not to his old-school, man-in-charge father. She blushed at fart jokes. She and her friends got old young. Marcia and her friends were determined to be young old. The passing of the baton.

Lo and behold, as if on cue, Marcia stood in the doorway. He hadn't heard her coming, so intent was he on his musings. She looked beautiful, thick dark hair, pale, adamantly sun-protected skin, simple white cotton nightgown. Where was it: the cold cream, the hair curlers, the womanly paraphernalia his mother had worn to bed? Where was it all? Where had it all gone, all that signature female stuff needed to shore up feminine appeal? Here stood this preternaturally lovely creature, firm and glowing. His wife. He got up and poured himself another Scotch and sat back down. She remained in the doorway.

"Are you sure that's a good idea—on an empty stomach?"

"Ah—wifely solicitude."

"Do you want me to fix you something?"

"No dear."

"David don't."

"Don't what."

"Do that dear stuff."

"Righty O."

"I'm worried about you."

"I'm touched."

"I mean it."

"I'm sorry," he said. "I certainly don't want to worry you."

"Maybe," she said, "you should try Prozac."

"I'm not depressed," he said. "I'm heartbroken."

He woke, still fully clothed, in the den when a little boy making vroom, vroom noises ran a small green truck across his tummy and then up into his hair. He felt stale, sweaty—it was going to be a scorcher. The door was still open to the outside and he could feel the heat coming in. He had a dull, thumpy headache.

"Hey baby," he said to Trevor. "Does Daddy look like a freeway?"

"Vroom, vroom," Trevor went on running the truck this way and that, up his arms and down.

"Hey Trevie," Marcia said coming into the room, "let Daddy get up. We're all going to be late here."

He looked at her. Slept like a baby, huh? She had on a tight turquoise T-shirt and skinny black pants, chunky slip-on shoes. That was it: she was part of the other tribe. That sassy, elemental tribe of survivors that now roamed the city, the ones he had seen out in force the night before. She had Kyle in her arms. They looked so pretty together with their matching dark hair and big eyes, Madonna and child. He picked up Trevor and sat him on his stomach. "Vroom, vroom," Trevor went, a big smile at his father.

"Come on you guys," she said, moving toward the kitchen, "breakfast."

"I hate you," David said. He said it softly and she didn't really hear.

"What?" she said, turning from the door.

"Nothing," he said.

"Daddy said he hates you," Trevor said, looking from one to the other.

"Daddy's just kidding," she said after a beat.

"Vroom, vroom, vroom," Trevor said.

The days got hotter and hotter, not the usual dry, desert hot, but soggy, almost East Coast hot. Everybody had a sweaty sheen on their skin. David was grateful for the heat. It gave him an excuse for his lassitude. He felt as if he were swimming through everything now. He'd come to, find himself talking to a client on the phone, engage for a minute and then fall away. Same at home. He had to fight hard to stay connected to the details, baths, feedings, kids' importunings for this or that—a story, a popsicle, a nighttime back tickle. He hummed a song to them, adding words: a back tickle, a popsicle, and then we all go to bed, and then we all go to bed. They giggled from their boy beds, little single dorm-room beds with ships' prows for headboards. The nautical conceit was heavy. Marcia had actually painted a bunch of ships, freehand, around the walls of both bedrooms. They had masts and tillers. There were schooners and dinghies, canoes and catamarans. For weeks, she had shoved picture books at David. What about this one? Do you like this? And then she sketched them on the wall in pencil while David sat on the floor, admiringly. Then she painted them. Late into the early mornings she painted, three weekends in a row, while he kept happy vigil, padding downstairs in his boxer shorts and T-shirt to get them more wine, checking on the boys, tucked into their big master bedroom for the duration of the project. It doesn't get any sweeter, he remembered thinking. That was summer, too, and it was hot. He got up behind her once, on the step stool, and put his hands around her, there in her Swiss cotton underwear, feeling her small, high breasts through the cotton—"I don't like silk or satin," she'd told him right off, maybe the first, certainly the second time they'd slept together. "It's corny." And she let him bring her down on to the floor and make love right there with the unfinished boats and paint fumes and when he woke up, hours later, she was back up there on the step stool adjusting some of the sails. Now the thought of any of that, certainly any thought of her elegantly understated underwear, made him nauseous, made him crazy, made him want to cry out. Try as he might, he could not keep himself from seeing that man take it off. He was taking it off thirty times a day and a hundred times at night. Off, off, off, gently, tugging, stripping, kneeling, off, off, off, peeling, pulling, stripping, off, off, off. It went on behind his eyes all the time, when he was talking to clients or driving in the car or singing to his boys—tickle, tickle, popsicle, and then we go to bed, and then we go to bed, a popsicle, a tickle, and then we go to bed. And all the while he smiled at them, his boys, his babies, and sang them to sleep, some strange man with big hands was stripping their mother. It was sickening. It was obscene. It was heartbreaking, the deft removal of that little bit of cotton, down over the thigh and calves and feet. He could see, he didn't want to see, but he could see, the damp place in her panties where they now lay on the floor. It was obscene. It was heartbreaking.

He had seen it begin—the verbal foreplay—in his very own house around his very own table. It was the usual Friday-night group. They rotated locations. At their house, then Karen and Marty's, then Gwen and Todd's. Three hard-core couples often with a stray thrown in, often Mary Lou, whose husband had taken off with a younger woman. She was their usual token single. Sometimes they left her out when nobody wanted to deal with her sometimes hilarious, high-pitched grief, her acerbic banter about the dating scene. Other nights they liked having her because her singleness made them feel safe and cozy. She wasn't on the list for the night in question but when David called Marcia and said he was stuck with a potential new client, in town from Philadelphia for just one night, owns a chain of drugstores, got to me through the Beechams, I can't not have him, she said, with resignation (because she didn't like surprise guests; he didn't either), "Then let me see if I can get Mary Lou."

Mary Lou was a sport, never acted offended when asked at the last minute. That was one of her major virtues. "Sure," she said and turned up looking particularly great: all leggy in a short black sundress, her close-cropped red hair tousled and bedroomy.

"Yum," Marty said, when she came in and Todd gave a wolf whistle. But the visitor, Web Allyn, didn't even really see her because he, David noted, was already sensorially attuned to his hostess. It happened right with the hellos, right at the front door, Marcia holding Kyle. Web smiling. OK, he thought. Might make snagging him and his account easier. No big deal. Men liked Marcia. He knew that. And this guy was hardly her type. He was big, a little soft and thick in the middle, hair a little too long, the alligator or whatever animal, cowboy boots. She would say later when they were deconstructing the evening: I liked him, he's different. But he's not my type (with a sharp, wistful laugh). And those boots.

They weren't sitting together—hostess and new guest. Marcia had put him between Mary Lou and Gwen, but he smiled up a lot from his courses, the cold red pepper soup with the cloud of crème fraiche in it, the chicken with endive and olives, the arugula salad, the meringue cake with raspberries.

"Jesus," he said, eating robustly, smiling at Marcia, "do you eat like this all the time?"

"All the time," David said grinning, Trevor draped around him.

"We do not. Come on, David, tell him the truth."

"All the time," he said solemnly, burying his nose in his son's soft hair.

They always had the kids these nights, everybody's kids. There was always a background gaggle of chirps and shrieks and tears. There was a teenage baby-sitter—sometimes two—who tried to hold the racket down and keep the kids in the other room, playing games, watching videos, anything, but they periodically drifted in and climbed onto a parental lap, falling asleep sometimes as their parents drank more wine and argued about movies or politics. These were their favorite nights, Marcia and David, especially the ones at their own house. They talked about the menu for days leading up to it, reading cookbooks in bed together. He always managed to get away early the night in question, stopping for the flowers on the way, always tulips, cream-colored if he could find them, pale yellow otherwise. Hair in a ponytail, wisps falling out, Marcia would fill the vases and carry them around.

"Whatdya think, here or here?" She moved them a half a dozen times.

"Looks great to me," he would say. "Go on up and change. I'll do the candles." They were always cream-colored, too.

"Check the crème fraiche," she'd shout down at him from upstairs. "Maybe we should fold a little fresh parmesan into it."

And then, with a rush, it would lurch into being: the evening. The door opening, their friends piling in, kids being arranged. The decibel level rising and rising with the early evening energy and the first cocktails 'til everyone sat, plates in front of them. And in the middle of it all, Marcia and David, at their opposite ends of the big polished cherry dining-room table, exchanging private signs about the food. He'd stick his thumb up, unnoticeable to anyone else, after a bite of the chicken or the meringue, or make a head-shaking, equivocal nod as he mouthed the word parmesan. She knew precisely what he meant: maybe they should have put some in the crème fraiche. Next time. Marital Morse code while around them their friends laughed and argued and ate. He tilted his eyes, just once, at their guest and Marcia threw him back an almost imperceptible nod. He's OK. We got lucky this time.

"I hated *Private Ryan*," Karen said. It was late. They'd just finished the dessert and her voice, wine-heightened, superseded other conversations. Everyone listened while Marcia, barefoot now, her long blue taffeta skirt swishing on the wood floor, brought demitasses of dark coffee in from the kitchen. Swish, swish. David swore he could hear it, the skirt sound, underneath the movie talk. Swish, swish. It was a sound he loved, a sound of well-being.

"Basically I did, too," David said.

"I thought it was pretty effective," Marty said.

"The opening and closing were unbelievably corny," Karen said. "And it was all so predictable."

"What does that mean?" Marty said.

"Come on," Karen said. "You know what we mean. The plot was contrived."

"All art is contrived," he said.

"Oh come on," Karen and David said, rolling their eyes.

"He's going heavy on us," Karen said smiling at her host. "Jesus, don't give him anything more to drink."

"Hey, what was that other movie I liked, the Vietnam one? Jesus, I can't remember anything anymore."

"Give me a hint," his wife said.

"Right," he said. "You know soldiers, the guys who torched the village . . . Come on. It's driving me crazy."

"I know the one you mean," Gwen said. "The one with, um, that really spooky guy."

"Oh yeah," David said, "Willem Dafoe."

"*Platoon*," Marcia said over her guest's head, as she leaned in to put down his coffee. He had said nothing.

"You're not much of a moviegoer?" she said close to his ear, as the others continued talking.

"No," he said.

David saw it and said: "Hey, Web, what did you think of it?"

"I didn't see it," he said.

"Neither one?"

"No, I don't like war movies."

The table went a bit still. There was a tension.

"Sorry," he said sensing it, looking up, a flicker of a smile.

"What kind of man are you?" Marty said in a mock-tough baritone.

"You guys aren't getting it," Marcia said, back at the head of the table. "You were in Vietnam, weren't you?" she said, speaking softly to her new guest.

"Yep," he said.

The "yep" lay there for a minute until David brightly disbanded the table. "Cigars and brandy outside," he said rising. "Women included."

"Like, duh," Mary Lou said, linking her arm through David's, slouching a little to do it.

He wasn't sure what happened next. He'd reconstructed the evening so many times in his head, he couldn't be sure of anything. Nothing dramatic happened. It was more trying to remember the absence of something or somebody: Marcia, Web. Web, Marcia. He and the regulars went into the garden after one or the other parent in each couple went to check on the kids. He did that, went to check their kids. The stalwarts were still involved in some video. That meant

Kyle, not Trevor, who'd fallen asleep on the floor in front of the TV. But there was Kyle, all bright-eyed and baby-faced and upright among the three older kids, their faces illuminated by the television screen. David carried Trevor to his bedroom. He looked so delicate still but in his father's arms he definitely felt heavier than even a month ago. It was still hot, so he just plunked him down on top of the covers in his tan shorts and blue and white striped T-shirt with dried chocolate ice cream all over the front. David inhaled deeply of him, his oldest son, his firstborn: chocolate and shampoo. Then back down he went and into the garden, where Marty was biting off cigar ends for a couple of the women.

"What a guy," David said, clapping him on the back.

"Well, if you'd get a damn cutter that was any good . . ."

"What and not have your spit all over our smokes," Mary Lou said.

At that point, Marcia started to leave . . . again? He was subliminally beginning to try to keep track.

"Hey Marsh," David said to her back, "can you bring me the cognac?"

She went and came back with the bottle and a trio of snifters in her hand. She handed them to him and went away again. He didn't have a lot of memory of her after that. He saw her moving around the table at one point, picking up plates—hey, he wanted to say, not now, we never do it now. That's a rule; we'll do it later when everyone's gone. Then he saw Web with some plates, too, the affable guest. Then—what?—he didn't see them again. She touched base some while later, looking flushed, triumphant, her thick, dark hair now twisted into a sloppy bun on top of her head.

"Christ," Marty said, "you outdid yourself tonight. Why don't you just cater all the meals. We'll pay you."

"To hell with you," Karen said.

"You're good, sweets," he said, patting his wife's leg, the calf, that's what he could reach from where he was sitting, reaching over

Mary Lou to do it, "but come on, Marcia here is the crème de la crème. Hey what was that stuff anyway—in the soup? I could eat that on everything . . . Yeah, yeah, don't say it," he said to Todd, who'd cocked an eyebrow.

She'd disappeared again. David thought about getting up, checking again on the kids, using the bathroom, something, but he didn't. He stayed in his place. Web came outside to say good-bye.

"Sorry to be the spoilsport," he said. "I'm still on East Coast time." He shook hands with everybody, saying, "Please don't get up, no, no, stay put." He made the circle. David was up and they were walking toward the door. Marcia came down the stairs at that moment, both men looking up. "What a great dinner," Web said, putting out his hand, Marcia taking it, not exactly a handshake. David patted him on his other arm, reaching up, Web turning to him then and saying he'd call him when he got back home in a week or so, still had other business stops. Then he was out the door. They stood looking at him walk to his car, but Marcia turned back toward the kitchen before David closed the door. He found her outside with the others.

"So," Mary Lou said, "is he married?"

"Divorced," Marcia and David said as one. Who had told her? Had he told her?

"They always have to bring up that war stuff," Todd said.

"He didn't bring it up," Gwen said. "And anyway, why not?"

"I'm just a little tired of it. All this World War II crap—the movies, the memorials. Just taking potshots at Clinton."

"Are you saying Clinton didn't evade the draft? I mean, that's just . . ."

"Hey you guys," Karen said. "Lighten up."

"Speaking of lightening up," Mary Lou said, "am I mistaken Todd, or have you put a few blond streaks in there?" She gestured at his hair. Todd laughed.

"Yeah," Marcia said, "I noticed, too."

"Where will this male vanity end," Karen said. "Next you'll be having liposuction."

"Not on your life," Todd said. "People die doing that stuff. We had a big malpractice suit in the office about it."

"No," Marty said, pinching his stomach. "I got it fair and square and I'm keeping it. Jesus that was a good meal."

"Hey creep," his wife said, "you already said that."

"Well if I'm repeating myself, you better take me home."

The men went upstairs to get the children, carrying down the sleeping ones, herding in front of them the older, still upright ones. At the door, there were hugs and kisses, last minute scrounging around for toys and purses, the usual warm, cluttered ending to their Friday evenings.

"Thanks for including me," Mary Lou said, planting a kiss atop David's head. There was no ironic zing about the last-minute invitation. She meant it.

"You're getting taller," he said, stretching to kiss her. "You look great."

"Maybe, but our guest warn't interested in me," she said, in a mock western accent. "Shore warn't."

"Well then," he said, "we won't let him come back."

When the door was shut, Marcia had already disappeared into the kitchen.

"Don't do it now," he yelled in. "I'll get up at six and get a jump on it."

"No need," she said, reappearing, "Juana's coming early. I just wanted to put the last of the food up."

They went upstairs and passed the boys' rooms, peeking in. Everybody asleep, Kyle's small breaths audible, the windows open. "Your new client liked my boats," Marcia said.

"Your boats?" David said. "When'd he see them?"

"I showed them to him. He was going on about the food and I said if you like the dinner you should see my boats."

And that's when she said the thing about thinking he was interesting but that he wasn't her type.

And those boots, she added with a laugh, taking off her swirly taffeta skirt. But she'd said something else about how their lives had been awfully immune from tragedy.

"What about Kyle?" he said.

"That was a tragedy averted."

"Isn't this something we should feel good about?"

"So how did the week go?"

They were back at Dr. Lou's, sitting in their same places on opposite ends of the sofa. It seemed to David as if they'd been coming here already six months. The doctor had on another, more intricately patterned colored sweater—roses and silvery blues with flecks of gold. No doubt they were his uniform. He had some image of himself: colorful but not too, assertive but soft, intricate. A little peacocky, David thought. No question, he'd had his eyes done. Maybe he'd also gone to a voice coach. People weren't actually born with these mellifluous baritone voices, were they?

"David?"

They sat. David said nothing.

"Marcia?"

"OK, I guess."

"OK—you want to try to flesh that out a little for me," Dr. Lou said warmly.

"OK means no drama, hysteria, crying."

"Crying isn't necessarily bad," Boo Hoo Lou said. That's the nickname David had suddenly given him. Boo Hoo Lou. It made him smile.

"David, you're smiling. What's that about?"

"Nothing. Just private."

"OK, you guys, let's try this another way. How's your sex life?"

"Is that a joke?" David said.

"No," Boo Hoo said. "It's not a joke. Marcia?"

"Nothing."

"What do you mean?"

"I mean there's nothing, no sex."

"Have you two made love since this happened?"

"Once," Marcia said. "It was pretty awful."

"Awful how?" Dr. Lou said.

"Do we have to do this?" David said. "I'm liable to get turned on."

"David, I know this can get uncomfortable. But if we don't get in here and root around, the wound will never get cleaned out."

"Bingo," David said smiling.

"You want to clue me in?"

"That's one of your phrases from TV, that cleaning-out-the-wound stuff. Marcia owes me $5. That was our agreement. Five bucks for any recognizable cliché. You want to pay up now, dear?"

"He's started this 'dear' stuff. I hate it," Marcia said. "He knows I hate it."

"Tell him that," the doctor said. "Look at him and tell him."

She looked down and around and finally at David. "I hate it when you call me dear. Don't do it anymore." There was a long pause and then a soft, "Please."

"As long as we're clearing the air here," David said, looking at her, "I'm supposed to look at her, right, Doc; I don't want to get this wrong . . . I don't like you running around screwing other men."

"We didn't sleep together," she said in a low, flat voice. "I tried to tell you that."

"What do you mean you tried to tell me? Then this is all some ghastly mistake and we can go home. Jesus, I'm relieved."

"Marcia," Dr. Lou said. "Did you tell him exactly what happened?"

MARRIAGE: A DUET · 113

"No, not exactly. He didn't want to know. He said he'd heard enough."

"In my experience, the imagination is worse than the truth. I'm sure David is imagining over and over any number of things, scenes, that could be dispelled if you just told him exactly what did happen."

David groaned. He couldn't stop himself. The bastard was pulling her panties off again. Maybe the doctor was right. Maybe he had to hear the gory details. Maybe it would be better that way—face the truth and get on with it. He looked up. "OK," he said to his wife, "shoot."

"Are you sure about this?" she said, looking at the therapist. "I don't really like this."

"You're in a safe place," he said with all that encouragingly soft wisdom David remembered from his TV appearances. Got to hand it to him. There's a reason he's America's Numero Uno marriage fixer. And weren't they lucky he just happened to live in their own back-yard. Oh, so lucky. What if he'd been in Atlanta or Houston or some-where instead of in the San Fernando Valley? "I just don't think you can get well until you get out the poison," Lou said. "You're as sick as your secrets."

David smiled broadly at his wife and held up five fingers, wiggling them in the air.

"That's ten," he said.

"All right, David, you're going to have to stop your games now if Marcia's going to be able to open up and share with you, really share, what happened."

"Righty O," David said, putting hand to forehead in a salute.

"I mean it," Dr. Lou said—now the stern TV taskmaster. "I can't encourage her to do this if you aren't going to be respectful and atten-tive."

There was a long silence. David looked at the bookshelves, down at the ground, then finally at his wife.

"OK," he said. "I will try."

"Try what?" Marcia said, looking at him. Did he see love? He did see love. He thought he saw love. But was it love he was seeing?

"To be attentive and—what was the other word?"

"Respectful," the doctor said.

"Respectful," he said, and he said it straight, encouraging her to begin.

What happened next was the worst thing that had ever happened to David, so far and away, that later he was amused if nonplussed at his ability to sit there and listen. He wanted to stop it, to stop her but as she got going he felt some diabolically prurient interest in her narrative. He actually felt, at one point, a stir of sexual appetite, something he had not felt for a month. That was when she talked about them getting into the backseat of the car. The transfer of bodies, the commitment to sex—car sex—was arousing. They'd had dinner, she said, at the trendy little bistro in the basement of her reconfabulated B&B near Dupont Circle. That's when she interviewed him. That was the pretext—or was it the subtext. David knew she had called Web from LA and set up a "meeting." She'd asked for his phone number after she got the assignment to do a profile on the woman who'd designed the Vietnam Memorial. David's nerve endings went on alert when she asked for the number, but what do you do? He didn't know. This was a first-time thing. You didn't go questioning your wife just on a whim of suspicion—or did you? Should you have? He'd never been in this position before. She went to Washington, her first major out-of-town work trip since Kyle. She'd laid her clothes out carefully on the bed the night before, holding them up and asking him, should I take this, or this?

"Washington's majorly stuffy still," she said, "I guess the skirts are better than the pants."

They talked each night she was away and she was up, bubbly, full of details—how her interviews were going, what women were wearing on the street (the young architect was "brilliant, but reserved, a cautious interview, but I think I can get more out of her"; the women on the street "dowdy beyond belief"). He knew she was going to see Web. He'd asked. She'd told him. Day three at first, then it became night three because he had to reschedule. She wasn't keeping anything secret. David knew they were having dinner. Which they did. And then—and this he only learned now at Boo Hoo Lou's—they decided to visit the memorial by moonlight. It was a chilly, full-moon night. They were bundled up, frisky and full of merlot. He took her hand and led her up and down the shiny, moon-splashed wall, introducing her to his dead friends. It was moving. It was great copy. It was foreplay.

Watching her talk about it, David saw the glint in her eye. Still. Now. After all the fallout. It was there. It was one of the romantic highlights of her life, archived now forever, and nothing was going to undo that. Nothing. They got back in the car. It was parked out of the way, in shadow. He reached to rub her cold hands between his. They kissed. They pawed. Shed coats. Undid buttons. It was frenzied, teenagey, exhilarating. She didn't have to say it. She showed it. David saw the determinedly impassive face of the good doctor. You bastard, he wanted to say, you get off on this stuff, don't you? No wonder you're in this trade. But nobody said anything except Marcia. She didn't remember whose idea it was to get into the backseat, but they did, intending, she said, to have sex. That was the, in the circumstances, idiotically clinical phrase she used: have sex. But neither had protection. So they had to settle for . . . her voice got even lower, she'd get it all out now, she was committed . . . oral sex. At which point, David whimpered. He was not one of those who thought a blow job less innocent than penetration (how about that for another clinical word?). Not at all. He found oral sex more intimate, more uninhibited. It had a kind of enforced tenderness to it, a required delicacy.

David reached over, picked up his suit jacket and draped it over his head. He could listen, but he couldn't watch that face anymore. That glint would drive him mad. He sat under there. He heard them whispering and then Marcia resumed.

"There isn't much more," she said. "That's all that happened. When I got back to the hotel, there were three messages from David. I knew if I didn't call him he'd keep calling all night long. So I called him. He asked where I'd been and what I'd been doing and I tried to lie, say we'd had dinner, then gone to hear some music, but he could hear it in my voice and finally just asked flat out if we'd had sex. And I said, more or less, yes. He asked if I was going to leave him and I said, no, it was just something that happened. Web and I—nothing else happened. We agreed to meet for breakfast. We talked. He wanted to, but I knew . . . there was too much at stake. I flew home that afternoon. The minute he picked me up, I told David how sorry I was and that I love him, but now it just feels like he's intent on punishing me."

"Tell him that," the doctor said. It was weird hearing another voice. For fifteen minutes, Marcia's was the only one audible in the room.

"Tell him what?"

"That you're sorry and that you love him."

"I do love him," she said.

"Tell him."

Apparently this was the preferred marriage reclamation technique—this mano a mano conversing. You tell her. You tell him. Look at him. Look at her.

David felt her voice directed toward him. "I do love you," she said. "I've told you that over and over. I just . . . I can't do this with him under that thing . . ."

"David," the doctor said in his best wheedlingly adult voice, one David recognized from his own parental repertoire. "Can you come out now?"

Under his coat, David was rocking back and forth silently. His arms were tight around his body.

"You have to be patient," the doctor said quietly. "This is a process."

"I'm trying," she said.

"You've shattered his trust. You have to work to regain it."

"Bing, bing," David said from under his suit jacket as he thrust both hands in the air, all ten fingers waving like mad.

In the days that followed their second visit, David began to understand something he thought he would never personally understand: how you came to live in your marriage and outside of it at the same time, tethered by hurt, disappointment, habit. The habit of mornings, of teacher conferences, of those expertly rendered dinner parties: the tribe of regulars, the cream-colored tulips, the crème fraiche (by all means, let's try the parmesan in it next time). It didn't take that long for these other things—disappointment, habit—to feel strangely like love while not being, to fill up the space, so that you could go on and by and by even laugh together again at the naiveté of your younger love-struck selves. They did that already, brusque, somewhat mirthless little barky laughs about their wedding-day earnestness. Do you remember that Yeats poem we read—about putting your dreams beneath my feet? Yeah, God, were we that corny? In time, David figured, the giggles would even take on real mirth, survivors' mirth. That, too, could feel like love. He'd known people, of course, who lived like that, a fair number of his clients who grumbled about their wives but had no intention of leaving them—or vice versa. He had a few rich, disaffected wives as clients—women who'd inherited money or, in rarer cases (though these were increasing) made it on their own. But they didn't confide as much, not in him; they had, undoubtedly, legions of friends and attendees like hairdressers to do that with. It was the men who talked to him, not always directly—in fact, seldom directly. It came through money. He had arranged condo purchases for mistresses, college funds for kids had out of wedlock, breast implants for the girlfriend of the moment, the money moved silently, like a fish under water, from here to there, from one account to another, and thence to the mortgage company or plastic surgeon, nothing traceable, nothing breaking the surface, not one dollar, not one penny. He was proud of his skill even as he pitied the players. He and Marcia went to their Christmas parties and he watched them, these husbands and wives with the various arrangements he himself helped facilitate (that word again), and he felt both just a little bit soiled and quite smug. The men said they weren't going to leave because of the kids or because they didn't want to divide up the spoils, but he watched them those party nights and he heard them when they complained to him on the phone and he knew they stayed out of some almost umbilical attachment to their marriages—even to the wives they hadn't had sex with in years. But he was not like that, not like them. He had not settled. He would not settle. He had the real thing.

Those nights after those parties he was amorous in the truest sense of the word. Marcia would go upstairs to check on the boys and he would drive the baby-sitter home. He loved the drive, the sweet anticipatory delay. They would drive down Wilshire—he and the young sitter of the night—making small talk, their breaths fogging the windows, exchanging groans as they passed the Christmas tree lots full of gaudy, pastel-dyed trees with their big white turd-plops of fake snow. One of them, a spikey-haired, would-be poetess with dark circles under her eyes, actually used that phrase about the snow—no doubt, she'd already stuck it into one of her literary offerings. On they'd drive into sleeping suburbia, a few lawn displays of candy canes and crèches still lit up, despite the late hour, and all the while, as they made Christmastime small talk—done all your shopping yet? Are you staying in town?—he'd be thinking, with increasing specificity, of his naked wife waiting at home for him in their bed. He would find her, sometimes in a cotton gown, sometimes naked, dozing already in a fetal curl, and he would lie down next to her, his erection pushing against her buttocks. She would uncurl, moaning back against him. She might stay that way, facing away from him. He could enter her that way. It was all sweet and sleepy and fluid. Sometimes she would come sharply awake and mount him and he could watch her, her eyes closed, moving with determined hunger, up and down, reaching to touch herself and bringing her fingers to his mouth. He had never, after meeting her, after sleeping with her, wanted anyone else. He felt, in fact, as if he'd never really wanted anyone before. He had had a few romances, thought he had known love, somewhat, but something in Marcia's directness, her pallor and litheness—those small high breasts, those sharp, almost adolescent hipbones—had excited him in some elemental, transportive way. She had about her a well-bred wantonness, a semi-coy salaciousness that made him—a rather cautious if wry numbers cruncher; that's how he thought of himself—wild. He did not mind her sexual self-sufficiency. The first night he went to her apartment to pick her up, he noticed, when she went to get her coat in the bedroom, that she kept her sex manuals right on the living room shelves. There were *Any Woman Can* and *Achieving Orgasm Every Time* tucked in with *Crime and Punishment* and *La Nausee*. He blushed when she caught him looking.

"You read French?" he said.

"That, too," she said, linking her arm through his. She was thirty-three when they met; he was thirty-eight. She was a writer—a bonus. He had wanted to be one himself, coming to LA after college intending to be a screenwriter, but drifted—given his natural ability with numbers—into managing the money of his friends who were actually making it in the business. He didn't mind, especially after meeting her. He shifted his focus: family first, work second, a means to an end. They talked that first night about having children—two, two or three years apart, even agreeing that two of the same sex would be preferable.

"We're destined," he said. "Most people would want one of each."

"I know," she said. "But they're not smart like us. Gotta have two of the same so they can be best pals."

"Absolutely," David said, marveling at their accord.

Within six months, they'd bought a house, moved, and gotten married in their very own exquisitely decorated backyard. In the days leading up to the ceremony, Marcia, on her hands and knees, was potting plants late into the evening. He swooned to see her so, his efficient, gifted wife to be. He felt as if he'd been waiting for her all of his life. He would do anything for her, anything to make her happy, anything to go on generating her X-rated bedroom exhalations. Their first Christmas together in the house, he showered her with the decorously titillating Swiss cotton underwear she favored.

"I should have known," he said, as she pirouetted in front of their small tree in her new undershirt and briefs, "that this stuff would turn out to be a lot more expensive than all that satin stuff."

"What other stuff?" she said teasingly, lifting the teddy over her head. "What do you know about all that?"

He knew. The women his clients had fixed him up with routinely wore it: navy blue satin boxer shorts, crimson silk push-up bras, brown lace thongs. No nonsense, career women in expertly tailored pantsuits would undress and there they'd stand in see-through bras and lace-trimmed crotchless panties. Hooker wear for the high-achieving. It was all faintly embarrassing and effortful (if often effective), he thought—certainly on the bodies of the biologically desperate, the thirtysomethings hoping to snag a husband/sperm donor—and certainly none of it carried the sting of virginal erotica that Marcia's underthings did. Everywhere he turned, from underwear to financial management—she immediately assumed their household account and was a demon at it, every bit a match for his budgetary skills—to hardware for the kitchen cabinets, she pleased him. Her choices did. His admiration grew, his sense of contentment, his sense of pride when they went out together or when friends came to their house.

"You lucky bastard," they would say to him in front of her. "What did you do to deserve this?"

What indeed.

"Tell her that. Say it. Tell her you don't—or didn't—deserve it."

Back they were in their respective corners on Dr. Lou's tasteful if faintly scratchy sofa. A week had passed. Autumn had come, the heat breaking, the first cooler days. Everybody was always saying there were no seasons in Southern California. There were. David loved the nuanced slide from one to the other. Who needs all that snow, all those garish autumn leaves, he'd say to his friends who still put down LA, the new refugees from the East. He had been one once, almost two decades ago now. He knew it was a waiting game, that time and sun would dispel their prejudices. It was the rare intransigent who could not be seduced. Trevor was back in school, kindergarten. He and Marcia had both taken him his first day, David in one of his pin-stripe suits, Marcia in exercise wear, an oversize cotton sweater and leggings, both chatting at him on the ride.

"You'll be fine, sweetie. Robbie will be here and Connie."

"Right," David added, "and that nice Mrs. Leslie we met when we visited." (Somehow teachers, he reflected, were among the only females—maybe the only—you could still call Mrs. or Miss instead of Ms.)

Strapped in one of the big, cushy back seats, Trevor was silent. He looked so small. David watched his narrow little face in the mirror and wanted to pull over, scoop him up, and keep him forever in a bear hug. Funny, he thought: all the safety precautions, the helmets and carseats and knee pads, the endless array of childproofing unheard of when we were kids. And you still couldn't protect them. Maybe it was all some sort of tacit acknowledgment of that. Trevor walked bravely into the classroom between his parents, not looking back when they left. In the car, Marcia burst into tears and David reached for her hand and held it, but let go at the first stoplight.

"She knows that," David said, moving around on Dr. Lou's sofa. Was it always this scratchy?

"Does she?"

"Is this some sort of Socratic dialogue? I thought we were just going to do some of our TV-land schmoozing." The guy never bit.

"You might try telling her."

"What—that I didn't deserve it?"

"Why not?"

"Because it sounds pathetic."

"Is that how you feel?"

"Oh, shit," David said.

"Marcia," the doctor said, "maybe you can help here? You don't think David's pathetic, do you?"

They looked at each other, husband and wife, and some mutual glimmer made them both laugh.

"See, she does think so," David said.

"But she's here because she loves you and she wants to work on the marriage." It was his TV pap. David liked driving him back into it. It cheered him right up, usually. But not this time. He was losing ground and he knew it. The jauntiness had gone out of his hurt.

"I don't like it here," he said in a small voice, sounding just like Trevor when they picked him up after his first day of kindergarten.

Marcia looked at him. She put her hand out but let it fall on the sofa between them. "Lou," she said, "what about Prozac?"

"You want Prozac?" he said.

"I mean for him."

"David," he said. "Is this something you're interested in?"

"Should I be?"

"I don't know. What do you think?"

"What do you think? Will it perk me up?" He was rallying a bit to the old Socratic sitcom sport. Badda-bing, badda-bang, badda-boom.

"It can jump-start things if someone's really mired in a depression, but I have to warn you, it does have some side effects."

"For instance?"

"Well, it can cause loss of appetite in some people and it can also cause a loss of sexual appetite."

"Do you," David said to his wife, "have a preference?"

Four days before, she'd awakened him in the night, mouth on a nipple.

"What," he said groggily. He was routinely taking sleeping pills now, one, sometimes two, washed down with Scotch. Usually, she just left him alone.

"You were snoring," she said, looking up at him. She was the old Marcia—warm and provocative and proficient. She moved down his body, but he pulled her up.

"You're right," she said, not missing a beat, beginning to straddle him, "let's have another baby."

It was surreal, optimistic and impossible. He couldn't do it, wouldn't do it, though he had an incipient erection. She rolled off of him and he rolled over to attend to her with his mouth. He could not not do it. Some reflexive desire to pleasure her overcame his anger— that plus a fear that if he didn't do it a certain someone else would. She came, small and contained, a crisp little mechanical come. When they were trying to get pregnant—just a matter of months for each boy; her usual efficiency, David thought—the pleasure was a whole other expansive thing. He had no idea it would be that way. He realized he had never made love to a woman without protection—her part, his part, everybody's part. That always took center stage at some very early point, at the first hint of beddableness: how not to get pregnant, how not to get a sexually transmitted disease. What are you using? Are you on the pill? Have you got a condom? One of the great reliefs of marriage was the not asking, the just doing. But even that had not prepared David for the added eroticism, the added sweetness of truly unprotected sex. No stopping and starting. No diaphragm. The thrill of their complete nakedness, his and Marcia's, Marcia whom he worshiped, Marcia, the would-be mother of his child, made of the sexual act something exalted, an act not just of pleasure but of potential creation. He had felt so free, so potent, so virile. It hadn't lasted long, that unprotected period, because she got pregnant so fast, but it had left a lingering glow in David's libidinal memory. Maybe she was right. They should go back there. Try to have another baby. He should lighten up. Get a grip. Stop being a drama queen (as Marcia, in irritation, had accused him of being after saying she had apologized already a hundred times). Try Prozac. It was only one isolated grapple, one little nighttime backseat blow job with the Vietnam Memorial casting its proximate moonlit glow on their coupling—all right, quasi-coupling. Aarrrgh, he cried out silently, at the image. Aarrrgh—wasn't that the word that cartoon characters used (but how many a's, how many r's?). Perfect word, David thought sitting there, a perfectly formed angular groan, all elbows of despair and frustration trying to get out of your throat. Wonder what genius first thought of it, sitting at his desk doodling around looking for just the perfect word to stick in one of those balloons over the head of some grumpily disconsolate dog (wasn't that it first, a dog who said it?) or human.

"Aarrrgh," he said out loud.

"What's that, David?" Dr. Lou said.

"Aarrrgh," he said again, softly this time, with a slight smile. "Isn't that a great word when you think about it . . . the way it's formed and . . ."

"David, sooner or later, you're going to have to stop this," Marcia said.

"OK," he said.

"OK, what?" Dr. Lou said.

"OK, I'll try the Prozac."

"If you're sure, David."

"I suppose it can't hurt," he said, adding, with a bleak smile, a punctuating "aarrrgh."

"OK, David. Maybe it will help. I can't write the prescription myself, but I'll call a psychiatrist I use and have him do it. I'll give you his number and you can call him later today. But only one condition."

"Let me guess," David said. "As long as we keep coming here."

Boo Hoo Lou eyed him over his half glasses, now in place so he could write the pill pusher's number. "Time's up," he said, scrawling on a pad and handing David a piece of paper. "Try to have a little fun," he said walking them to the door, one multicolored cashmere arm around each of them, a quiet whiff of aftershave. "Dig down and try to remember what first drew you to each other," and as David turned to face him, he said, preemptively, with a slight smile: "Bingo."

That first hint of fall was brief, misleading. The October days now exploded into a 90-degree-plus Indian summer. David took to leaving the office early and going to get Trevor at school and heading directly to the beach without stopping home. He carried their bathing suits in his briefcase and father and son changed in the dank, urine-smelling little stalls in the public bathroom, chatting at each other as they raced into their trunks.

"I'm going to be first."

"No Daddy, no Daddy. Me." He'd hear his son, giggly and breathless on the other side of the flimsy metal partition.

"Here goes Daddy, he's down to his boxers, he's got them off, he's got one leg in his suit, oh no, here he goes, the other leg . . ."

"No, no, Daddy, I'm going to beat you, I'm going to beat you."

Triumphant and noisy, Trevor would appear under his stall, scampering under the door, a soggy little bit of toilet paper clinging to one knee, and grabbing his father around the legs.

"It's me," he'd say. "I won, I won, I won."

"I don't know. I think it's a tie," his father would say, lifting him up.

"No, no, Daddy, I won, I won," Trevor would shriek into his chest. "You know I won."

In their matching rubber flip flops, they'd take their clothes back to the car. David would hang his suit carefully, put Trevor's school clothes on the seat, then get the umbrella and boogie boards from the trunk. They padded down the clean, wide beach together holding hands, each with a board—and in David's case, the umbrella as well— tucked up under the other arm, casting man-boy shadows. At the little rise just before the high-tide line, they made their place, putting up the umbrella, lining up their towels side by side and then putting sunscreen on each other. David did most of the anointing, but Trevor loved to do his father's back.

"I'm spelling my name now," he'd laugh from behind his kneeling father. "T-R-E-V-O-R."

The beach on a fall afternoon—even a hot one—was almost completely deserted. "This is our very own beach," David would say. "I've arranged for everyone to stay away but the pigeons."

"Did you really do that, Daddy?" his son asked.

"Absolutely," David said.

"How did you tell them all?" Trevor asked.

"I called them on my cell phone."

"Daddy," he'd say, but David would by then be running toward the water with his boogie board.

"Last one in is a rotten . . ."

"Egg," Trevor would scream rushing by him into the water.

They'd paddle in the shallow water on their boards, looking up at the palisades and the palm trees standing like well-ordered sentries in the afternoon light. Trevor would count them from one end of the high bluff to the other and back.

"You missed that one there," David would say pointing.

"No, Daddy, I got that one."

"Well how about that one then, six in from the right."

"I got that one, too," he'd say.

"A bean counter just like your dad."

"No silly, not beans, trees," Trevor would say and laugh. If the waves weren't too big, they'd sometimes leave their boards on the sand and swim out a little farther, the son on his father's back. David was a very strong swimmer—he'd competed in high school—and his little boy clung to him as they caught a wave.

"Here we go," he'd say, "hang on," feeling Trevor cling tighter, David with a firm grip on top of Trevor's own grip. "Whee," they'd scream together. "Whee."

"Again Daddy," his normally skittery little boy would say the minute they bumped onto the shore. "Please, please."

And out they'd go again. And again. Then they'd lay together on their towels, shivering for a moment 'til they got warm. Sometimes, if the wind had come up, they'd dive right into the sand.

"Brrr," David would say, burrowing.

"Brrr," Trevor would say, squiggling down beside his father and they'd tunnel their hands through the sand until their fingers touched and Trevor would shriek with delight when they did.

Lying in the warm sand, the sun on his face, his son's fingertip palpitating against his, David would sometimes drift off. The sweetest sleep, everything muting, slipping away into the sound of the waves and the squawking gulls, the smell of sun lotion and salted air and toasted cigarette butts, a sensory tangle that would tug him down below consciousness. Then Trevor would be gently touching his chest (not like Kyle who would raucously leap upon him), his face.

"Daddy, Daddy, you fell asleep. Mommy will be mad if we're home too late." But Mommy wouldn't be mad. Mommy wasn't holding the high cards anymore. But the mention of her broke David's drowsiness, like snapping a stick in two. He came up out of his nap hard and sad and had to fight it, straining to smile into his son's innocent face. David dawdled, holding Trevor against him, then turned impish, raining a fine drizzle of sand onto his son's cradled head.

"No Daddy, no," Trevor pulled up, David letting him, holding him in only a pretend restraint. "You've made a big mistake, mister," Trevor said.

David could not help laughing. The mister always got him. Trevor used it when he was being his mock tough self. A handful of sand drizzled onto David's tummy. That's all: no throwing, no fistfuls.

"I told you, mister," Trevor said, trying to look stern, furrowing his small brow up at David, giggling while trying not to giggle.

"Mister," David said, "thinks it's time for little boys to wash the sand off," and in a deft move, he was up, Trevor against his chest, bounding toward the water. He hesitated, giving his son a chance to say no, then plunged ahead, hurdling the small waves with Trevor wrapped around his neck. "Count to three," he said, "and we'll dunk."

"One, two, three," they screamed together, and under they went, coming up head soaked and blowing and David, catching sight of the bluff and the palm trees, son in his arms, thought: OK, this is it. I'm going to have to get over it.

But as he and Trevor—chatting like a happy little noise box beside him: "Daddy, let's get a huge float that we can use together tomorrow. Tommy has one for his pool and maybe some flippers, that would be . . . Do you think we need to bring Kyle . . . Mommy says he's going to start being sad . . ."—wound their way deeper and deeper back into the early evening traffic and the noise and the city, up away from the beach and close to home, closer and closer, he felt sick again, silly and small and unbrave and humiliated. Something tightened in his chest. Maybe that's what the Prozac did, if and when it kicked in, unloosed the knot. He'd been taking it for a week and nothing had happened. They had, the psychiatrist had told him on the phone, a whole pharmacopoeia of goodies to try if this didn't work, so he should not despair. One day at a time. Apparently that bracing exhortation had wormed its way into the bromidic lexicon of even the most rigorously trained shrink. David was actually smiling a little at the memory, picturing the tweedy, graying Freudian—or Jungian or whatever he was—on the other end of the phone who was, without setting an eye on him, perfectly happy to give him pills—and pap— which he, in wounded turn, was only too happy to swallow.

"Daddy, you weren't even listening," Trevor said.

"I was, too," David said.

"No you weren't," Trevor said.

"You were talking about getting a float and flippers and maybe bringing your little brother. See?"

"But what about the bobs?"

"Oh shit," David said. "I totally forgot."

"Daddy, you said a bad word."

"That'll be our little secret, right," David said, turning the car around and heading back to the fish market.

"You should have said something sooner," David said, teasingly.

"I did, Daddy. You weren't listening."

They pulled into the fish market to get the shrimp for the "bobs." They were the kids' favorite: shrimp kabobs with pieces of peppers and onions. They loved making them with their parents, unwinding the wire hangers with their dad, threading on the food with their mom, everybody being careful, careful, everybody laughing, standing around the barbecue while they cooked, then pulling the hot food off—Daddy's job because he had the big mitt. He got a new one every Christmas, birthday, and Father's Day, Marcia saving all manner of boxes, big and little, shirt boxes and stereo boxes, so the kids could wrap the mitts up, screaming with excitement as he opened them up, their contrapuntal little voices: "Whatdya think it is, Daddy? Whatdya think it is?"

"It must be a new shirt," David would say, judging from the box. Or: "A new stereo! My, my, how could you guys afford this?"—the kids bursting, a crescendo of giggles as David pulled off the ribbon and the wrapping paper and then peeled back the tissue and delicately put his hand down in.

". . . not a stereo, no, I guess not, it's not hard, like that, I can't imagine what it could be, too little for a shirt, this is a mystery," the kids now clambering on his back, peering down into the box with him, over him, beside themselves—"hurry, Daddy, hurry"—and then out it would come, by which time, they'd all be yelling, three male voices: "A mitt, a new barbecue mitt," David putting it on his hand and waving it around.

"And it fits just perfectly."

"You knew it Daddy, you knew it," Trevor would scream.

"Yeah, you knew it," Kyle would imitate, Marcia snapping picture after picture, so that they had a whole scrapbook reserved for mitt openings and sometimes when one or the other of the kids felt crummy or sad or had a cold, they'd get out the mitt book and relive it all together. He wanted to crawl into that book and he wondered if it would have been better if she'd just not told him, lied to him instead. Was the truth so valuable? There seemed to be such emphasis on it now, on everybody spilling their guts in public and groveling for abso- lution. It was the new national pastime. Was it really right to be able to buy yourself out of your misdeeds with a few mea culpas? There was something cheap about it, dishonorable. Maybe, David thought, the alternative was actually better. Maybe secrets were fine. Maybe a little deception went a long way. He wanted to unknow what his wife had done in the backseat of the car with everything in him, unsee her in that supine, semiclothed posture, her usually direct gaze lidded with pleasure. They had it all wrong, didn't they, completely back- ward? You weren't as sick as your secrets. You were as sick as your truths.

When they got home, it was almost six. The front door immediately opened. Kyle flew down the walk on his chubby three-year-old legs, all baby-voiced fury: "Where have you been, Mommy and me worried and worried."

Trevor was already out of his seat running the other way, past Kyle, toward his mother in the open doorway, shouting gleefully: "He used the 'S' word. Daddy used the 'S' word."

"Shrimp," David said coming around, brandishing a package. "The 'S' word."

"No Daddy. You know which one."

By now, David had picked Kyle up and Marcia was holding Trevor, the little traitor. He was no longer his dad's pal, his best buddy, his comrade in beach bravery. He was a little boy in his mother's arms. She was holding the high cards, after all. She was, standing there, radiantly maternal, holding his son hostage. Where in the world would David go? Where could he go? Her secret was safe with him. She'd counted on that. And she hadn't pushed it, hadn't run amok and had a full-tilt affair and really jeopardized her marriage. No. She was even efficient at adultery. A titillating little romp she could use for years to come for fantasy fare, a memory to leverage her libido in the dark of night when David couldn't stir her—a useful erotic flashback.

"I lit the barbecue a while ago," she said. "You'll probably have to stoke it up."

"Stoke it up," he said, kissing Kyle's forehead. "That's what we'll do, right boys? No wait, I have to do the hangers first."

"Kyle and I already did them, didn't we sweetie?"

"With the pliers. Mommy let me hold them."

"That Mommy's really something," David said.

They drank a bottle and a half of pinot grigio between them while they barbecued and then ate outside around the candlelit redwood table, each handling a child, helping to pull the food off the wire hangers. It was warm out, excited boy chatter filling the silence. There were small pots of communal butter for the shrimp and the kids dunked messily with everything—fish, bread, fingers—growing greasier in the candlelight. David suggested they bathe not upstairs but in the small outdoor wading pool, still up from the afternoon. Marcia did not object. She was a sport, this mother, overcoming her normal tidiness when it came to the kids (as with sex). David liked that about her, the surprise of her sportingness though he knew, with his bath suggestion, he was pushing her limits. But she stayed at ease. He couldn't rile her. She was letting him push a few limits, hoping— he knew this—that he'd find his way back through his minor asser- tions. Big, brave daddy bathing his kids in an outdoor pool. David stripped and ran toward the pool, splashing and shrieking. He sat in the cool water and waited for his kids. Marcia helped them out of their shirts and shorts and they came, two little naked males, small penises bouncing, toward their father. Marcia disappeared inside and came back with two pots of boiling water to add to the pool.

"Out of the way, men," she said, delicately pouring.

She handed David a bar of soap and as she did, he felt momentar- ily shy around her, grumpy. The wine was wearing off. He washed the boys, even their hair, eliciting laughter and then some squawks of protest and finally tears when the soap got into their eyes—Kyle's eyes, bringing his mother to wrest him up out of the pool with a towel.

"OK, that's enough," she said, hustling Trevor out, too, and herd- ing them inside and up the stairs. David lingered for a moment in the water, looking at his house, hearing the boys' protests, seeing Marcia move back and forth in front of the bedroom windows as she readied each for bed. They were tired so it was relatively easy to get them down. David heard no major tussles, no high-decibel last stands against sleep. Marcia's voice was tender and firm—mother-perfect, he thought. He got out of the water, wrapping up in the dark green terry cloth robe she had so thoughtfully—screw her!—brought down for him. He poured another glass of wine, turned off the patio lights and sat on the chaise in the darkness. Marcia came, stopping by the table to get her own glass, then sat down beside him, scooting him over with her behind. She, too, had on a robe, lightly belted and he could see, when she leaned to put down her glass on the flagstone, that she had nothing on underneath.

"Listen," she said, "can you try not to be snotty with me around the kids? It's OK when it's just the two of us, but I think they're beginning to pick it up."

"Really," he said. "How could I be so thoughtless."

"David, how long are you going to keep this up?"

He sat for a while, then said: "Tell me, Marcia, why did you do it?"

She was quiet for a long time. He tilted his head back and looked at the stars. He loved these warm nights. They were rare in Southern California. Light from the outdoor yard lanterns flickered on the water of the wading pool. His mouth was still greasy from the butter.

"I think I was just tired of being good," she said finally. "I've always been so good."

They were both quiet again and then she said, "You've always had me on such a pedestal."

"Sorry," he said, accenting it with a tight, one-syllable laugh, short and hard around the edges.

"I didn't mean to hurt you," she said softly, her hand now rubbing his thigh up under the terry cloth. "It wasn't a big thing." He looked at her now and could see, in her demeanor, the shift toward sex. Eyes bright, fingertips alert as they now, deftly, reached the base of his cock. He closed his eyes again because he didn't want to see her face—the telltale eagerness that might, if he wasn't careful, drive him right back into the backseat of that car—because he thought maybe they'd pull this off, some re-consummating lovemaking, and then move on. But it was no use. For the first time since he had met her, he could not maintain an erection. She kept up her manual ministrations. His penis swelled to half-mast, but would inflate no further. She finally gave up. He opened his eyes. She had reached over and picked up her glass and was upending the last of her wine.

"It's no big deal," she said, getting up. She smiled, looking, he thought, very calm and very beautiful as she tightened the belt around her white cotton robe. "By the way," she said, "we're due at Gwen and Todd's Friday, if that's OK. I need to let them know." With that she was gone.

He felt chilled, but couldn't move. His legs felt heavy, unmovable. He wanted to go get a Scotch but he could not seem to get up. No big deal, she had said. She had moved into the ranks of the all-understanding wives whose husbands, for one reason or another on one occasion or another, couldn't fuck them. A new sorority. Aren't we magnanimous? Sitting there immobilized, he hated her magnanimity almost as much as he hated her adultery. Didn't she see? It was not OK. Not even close to OK. It was a big deal, a huge deal. It was a tragedy. It had never happened before. He had never not been able to make love to his wife, never, not once. Just the sight of her had always stirred him. No longer. Now she was unable to arouse him with a full-court press. It had all turned complicated and he suspected that she liked that, the fact that it had become complicated, that she thought there was something maturing about it, sexy, grown-up, deep. They were in the muddy swim of things now. They had a marriage counselor. He was taking Prozac. He heard her talking to her girlfriends with a kind of excitable ruefulness. And she kept looking pretty, prettier and prettier—to him anyway, luminous in her semi-repentant naughtiness. They'd moved on, taken on complexity. His very impotence was proof of that. She had rendered him slack. She was no longer the good little girl; they were no longer the happy little couple. For all her mea culpas, she had never really recanted, never said she wished it had not happened. He'd seen the glint in her eye in that smarmy bastard's office as she recounted her escapade and the tender, beneficent look she'd cast him tonight walking away from his unexpectedly uncooperative cock. Even that was just a little bit exciting, wasn't it? A new scene to play. And really what kind of tragedy was it? Wasn't he just being melodramatic, as charged? Here he was on a comfy chaise in his thick robe in his beautiful backyard, two healthy little boys asleep upstairs, stars shining down from on high, just one more long-married, well-off, middle-aged guy who couldn't get it up. It was the stuff of every two-bit sitcom. A man couldn't have a tragedy anymore. The culture didn't allow it. They would deflate it with a laugh track—or inflate it with Viagra, which even someone as supposedly upright (ha, ha) as the acerbic former VP of the United States of America was going around hawking. Wink, wink. I can't get it up either. No, you could just forget it. There was no sorrow—literal or figurative—that couldn't be deftly handled. Tragedy had been banished from the realm.

He finally got up. By the clock in the den it was 11:14. He'd been sitting outside for almost two hours since she'd left him and he was deeply chilled now. He poured a big, neat Scotch and sat down on the sofa. He thought about some late-night TV, but it didn't help, hadn't helped during his other troubled nights. The noise just made him jumpy. He riffled around on the coffee table for a magazine, something mindless to leaf through 'til the liquor warmed and muted his brain, and found, in a stack of paperbacks, Dr. Lou's signature best-seller: *New Beginnings*. He flipped through the chapters, marked, he could see, in his wife's careful hand—this from a well-educated writer. He actually laughed. The whole world had gone mad. He stopped at the chapter called "The Romantic Illusion." It was the doctor's considered contention that romance was a dream-state, addictive and transitory. Only a child would cleave to such a notion. The gift of adultery—that was actually a phrase: "the perverse gift of adultery," he wrote, "is to blow open this illusion and allow the couple to see each other, warts and all, without the rose-colored glasses of romance. Then a deep, mature, loving relationship can grow up out of the ashes." He picked up the felt-tip pen that was on the coffee table and slashed and doodled all over the page, then added a few obscenities for good measure. He'd heard this stuff on the airwaves and always felt sorry for the people who were swilling it in, all those lonesome, shit-on souls who were looking to be made to feel better. He wasn't going to be made to feel better. He wasn't going to go back to the good doctor. And yet it really didn't matter, did it? It was already done. He and Marcia had already crossed over into some new territory—rather she had. He could see it clearly now through his Scotch buzz. She had sailed on ahead, leaping off her pedestal into this new so-called marital maturity, just waiting patiently for him to join her. But in that new world, what would he do with his great big valentine of a heart? Give it to his kids. He'd been doing that anyway; now there'd just be more of it for them. Maybe that's what they were all doing, his friends and a lot of the men he saw around him who were so preeningly paternal. Not just in a photo op way either, not just toting their babes around in backpacks or front packs or on their shoulders—though, God knows, there was a good bit of that. But it was more: diapering and carpooling and nuzzling them to make them laugh or rubbing their backs when they were scared. None of that stiff-upper-lip stuff that David remembered from his own childhood, not for these children—not even the boys. Oh no. Their daddies would be right there to coddle and cuddle them. And not under protest. These men did not have to be prodded by their aggrieved, overworked spouses. They embraced the task, the nuzzlingly heroic, protective, paternal task, not because they'd all suddenly discovered their inner father, not because they all remembered the male martinets in their own pasts and were determined to do it differently, but because they had this love to spare, this big goofy noble love their wives no longer wanted. His apparently didn't. It was passé. He was passé.

When he finally did join Marcia in bed, she rolled over and put an arm across his chest.

"It's probably just the Prozac," she said sleepily.

"At least it's working on one organ," he said.

The weather did finally turn and it turned for good. The heat, the real heat, was no doubt gone for the year and with its absence, David's mood darkened even more. A couple of coolish, gray mornings, he actually stayed in bed 'til ten. Marcia covered for him with the kids ("Daddy's got a lot on his mind," he'd hear her say softly to Trevor. Or, "Daddy's not feeling well.") while Mindy, his young female assistant, had instinctively slipped into a similar role at work, fencing off his inquisitive colleagues. ("He's putting in a lot of time at the kids' schools," he'd hear her say, sotto voce to someone on the office intercom. "You know, he's such a great father.") He realized that's the way his life felt to him now: overheard. There was now this cabal of whisperingly protective females between him and the world, hovering over the deflated form of the wounded male. It must be encoded in the genes, the gender. Mindy, after all, was fifteen years younger than he—a high school graduate with bleach-blonde spikes and huge gold earrings that banged against the telephone receiver. But she did it as naturally as the well-schooled Ms. Marcia. Did they like it? Did it make them feel important, needed, this time-honored work, this hovering intercession? Man on the ground; we'll take it from here. We'll get him up—every entendre doubled. Mindy did at least try to camouflage her commiserative looks. But every now and again, when he passed her desk and she looked up suddenly before she could shutter her gaze, he would catch the abject sympathy in her eyes—not the respectful sympathy accorded a man injured by another man, but the pitying sympathy given to a man injured by a woman. Once he got by her, got by all of them and into his office, the door shut, he was usually OK with the actual work. He could still focus on the numbers—

thank God for that—and be drawn into their tidy, linear universe where things added up. Yes, financial judgment was called for and some usual hand-holding diplomacy with his upper bracket clients, but he took a kind of perverse pleasure now out of sparring with and fawning over them in one brief, telephonic exchange—a deft one-two swat of insult ("What genius gave you that shitty tip?") and obsequiousness ("Gee, I wish I'd thought of that; I'll get right on it."), telling Marcia when she asked how work was, Marcia, who did finally, he was pleased to note, have a look of concern behind her new, radiant, post-adultery calmness, that the jerks didn't even seem to notice the change.

"I wasted all that niceness on 'em," he said.

"Maybe it's time," she said, "to call the doctor and try another antidepressant."

"Gee, I wish I'd thought of that," he said. "I'll get right on it."

And then on one absolutely stunning October morning just after dropping Trevor at school and Kyle at day care, David felt tears running down his face as he drove to work. They weren't noisy. They were just there, as if he'd sprung a leak. He dabbed at them with the back of his jacket. He didn't feel particularly bad. He didn't feel anything. But they wouldn't stop. They were somehow more alarming in their silence than his guttural sob in their maiden visit to you know who. He turned the car around and headed home. He would call in sick. He hadn't done that yet, he'd kept right on working, so he figured he was OK. So what if a few rich jerks didn't get richer today— or their mistresses or wives couldn't be immediately financially placated. He parked a half a block from his house and walked quietly around the back, hoping to avoid Marcia in her front office. He felt like an intruder sneaking up the stairs. He went into Trevor's room and lay down on top of the small bed, fully clothed, shoes still on, the boats scudding across the pale blue walls, flittering through his tears.

Quite a pleasing effect really. He watched them for a long time. They were hypnotic. He heard the phone ring, heard Marcia laugh, faint and faraway. She was still working on the article, fixing it. The editor liked it, she'd told him, just wanted a few more quotes. Quotes from whom? He didn't ask. She didn't say. It was clear she was pleased. There would be more work. All that she had brought to bear on her life with him she could—and would if it came to it—bring to bear on her life without him. He knew that now if he hadn't really known it before. Was a man supposed to be comforted by that—by the prospect of having not a needy, cloying, demanding ex-wife but a fully capable, independent one? Was that progress?

He must have fallen asleep because he came to smelling something good close by, right there. The smell brought him up from a deep dream he couldn't remember. Marcia sat beside him on the floor with a tray, a grilled cheese sandwich and a bowl of tomato and rice soup—the standard family comfort meal, all components always on hand for *whoever* should fall by the wayside. The boys with sniffles or fevers. David with the occasional lower back pain. Marcia with bad menstrual cramps. Her hand was on his forehead.

"You OK?" she said. "You don't feel hot."

"What time is it?"

"Twelve-thirty."

"Jesus. I never even called the office."

"It's all right. Mindy called here. You're covered. She said she'd call if anything major came up. I've got to run and get Kyle from Mrs. Marsden's."

She got up. He noted her usual grace.

"Eat it," she said, pointing at the food. "You need it. I'm going to run by the market after I get Kyle. You want anything?"

"Not that I can think of."

"Do you want to take off that suit? I'll drop it at the cleaners and get it pressed."

Then she was gone, down the hall. She'd blown into the room, beacon of health, food on a tray, and now, with determined normalcy, she'd disappeared back into the world of wellness, wanting to take his suit with her. It was breathtaking. He heard her in the bathroom, water running, then her footsteps coming toward him again. She stuck her head in the room, hair tied back, pale lipstick reapplied.

"No suit?" she said.

What could he say: I love you. I hate you. I can't take off this suit right now.

"I've really got to run," she said. "I think I'll stay out long enough to get Trevor at three."

"OK," he said. "Thanks for the tray."

"No big deal," she said.

"I'll miss you," he said, but she was already halfway down the stairs when he said it.

He lay there for another half hour, very still. The food grew cold and stopped sending up any cozy smells. Outside the window, the maple tree was shedding its big, brittle red, yellow, and orange leaves. He and the boys would rake them later, crunching them under their fat, rubber-soled running shoes. Ridiculous these shoes, ridiculously expensive and ridiculous—on the boys particularly—so swollen and elaborate with zigzags of rubber and netting and little floaty gel things in the heels. Doubled the size of their little boy feet. But everyone wore them now—men, women, children the world over. He remembered some pictures from Africa of these beautiful, fierce-looking young men in floaty tropical shirts brandishing machetes they'd apparently, according to the caption, recently used to hack up their neighbors. Even they were wearing Nikes. He'd caught the telltale logo on the shoe of the guy kneeling in the front of the photo and could never after, when seeing it, not think of him, all handsome and homicidal and grinning there in his Nikes. From then on, he bought the boys other brands. He didn't wear them either. He had—what did he have? Lying there he couldn't remember. He had three pairs, at least, including the really beat-up ones. But what were they? Reeboks? New Balance? No, that other one . . . He would go see. That's what he would do. He'd put them on with his floppy sweatpants. He'd call Mindy and see if there was anything urgent. He'd get something to eat—maybe try to resurrect the cheese sandwich somehow. Microwave? Grill pan? Maybe he'd have a beer with it. He'd be all ready for the boys' home-coming, standing in the yard, smile in place, rakes in hand. Daddy. But he felt so drowsy again, so heavy-limbed. And then the boats started to move—a mixed-craft regatta—and he realized the tears had once more started because his shirt collar, still unloosened around his neck, was damp. He knew he needed to stop feeling sorry for himself. But he wasn't really feeling sorry for himself. That wasn't it. He was feeling sorry for his marriage. He had loved it so, the sacred, shiny unit of it—what it felt like to be in it, what it looked like to others—and if he was going to stay in it, he was going to have to get over that love. One day at a time. Wasn't that what they all said?

"So you guys doing better?" Dr. Lou looked radiantly tanned, more full, David thought, of silver-haired, aren't-I-aging-well verve than ever, giving off the faint aroma of performing shrinks. He'd been away for a couple of weeks and had just come back, he told them, from an adultery junket—that was David's translation—in South Africa. Marriage counselors from all over the world meeting in Cape Town. Beautiful place, he said. Fascinating people. David saw him there in one of his sweaters—his SoCal therapist's plumage—giving his spiel before an auditorium full of multicultural marriage "facilitators" in Mao jackets and saris and tropical shirts. What did they do at night, these therapists, network and interface—and flirt? After all, they had the mechanisms of forgiveness already in place. Shame to waste it.

"We are doing better," Marcia said. She smiled at her husband. Four days ago, he'd finally stopped sleeping in Trevor's room, his son beside him on the pull-out trundle bed. Father and son having a sleep-over. Kyle was jealous so Marcia had spent a night or two on his floor on a futon. The modern American family.

"I guess I'm just another poster boy for Prozac," David said. He, too, smiled. Dr. Lou smiled.

"I don't think that's the whole story," the doctor said. "You have done some hard work here."

More smiles.

"Does this mean you've resumed your sex life?" he asked.

"Not exactly," Marcia said.

"No?"

"We tried," she said.

"I guess I'm not quite up to it," David said, sorry he'd suc-cumbed, realizing that Dr. Lou had long since heard every penile pun in the book.

"Is it a cause for concern?" he said.

Nobody said anything.

"Marcia?" he said.

"No. I don't think so. David's feeling better so that's the most important thing."

"David, I assume that means you want to stick with the Prozac."

"I guess so," he said. Truth was he was scared to get off it, which is why he'd agreed to come back here. It had finally started to work—that's how it felt anyway—about ten days earlier. His crying jags had abated. The sorrow had not exactly gone away. It had just somehow moved out of him and gone to sit over there where he could still see it, but it wasn't anymore buried within his own chest like a hatchet. It reminded him of when he'd had morphine after having his appendix out. The pain just floated up out of his lower belly and went and sat in the visitor's chair by the window, where David could see it but not feel it. That's how he felt now. He could function again, more or less: work, eat, play paddle tennis with Marty, talk dinner plans with Marcia. But he couldn't make love. And it wasn't like before when everything felt so raw and angry. Now it just seemed as if his libido had moved out along with the pain and they were off somewhere huddled together having a friendly chat. Sometimes David actually saw them sitting together on the plaid settee in his office, pointing at him. The imagery was overwhelming enough that he was tempted to share it, but caught himself just in time so as not to invite a probing response. Who wanted that at this point? David was a drug man now—go for the quick fix. He'd heard enough in this room to last a lifetime.

"You could try Viagra," Dr. Lou said, speaking the word tenderly, one man to another.

There it was, the other magic bullet for the broken-down male finally making its appearance. David realized that he had been expecting it.

"Why not?" David said out loud.

The other two looked at him, gauging his reaction. Did he mean it or was this a prelude to some outburst. He looked back. He did feel something taking form down inside—the old barbed hurt, a smart-ass retort—but it was as if someone or something (the Prozac?) reached up and patted him on the head. There, there, take it easy. It's all OK. Across the room, his libido and his pain were slapping hands in a high five. He blinked.

"David, is this something you want to try?" the doctor asked. "No one wants to push you into anything here."

"Can you take both at once?" Marcia asked, looking from the therapist to her husband and back again. "That's OK?"

"Yes, there's no contraindication. We'd start you on the lowest dosage and see how it goes."

"David?" Marcia said. "Are you really game for this?"

"Why not," he said again. "We measure success one erection at a time."

Dr. Lou rolled his eyes—a big, good-natured, Hollywood-sized eye roll—which Marcia answered with one of her own. David was once again sorry he'd succumbed. The bad guys were gaining advantage.

He was silent on the way home. There was a deep rosy sunset over the darkening hills, a few charred by the recent fires during the last heat wave—a melodramatic naturescape with a jammed freeway snaking through the middle of it. LA at rush hour. Marcia was driving, but she kept stealing glances at him, causing her to brake abruptly a couple of times when her eyes returned to the road. He said nothing. He felt her eyes on the side of his face but didn't turn.

"Is this a great county or what?" he said, shutting the car door when they got home.

Two days later was Halloween, which happened to fall on a Friday, their Friday again, the usual crowd expected. For the previous couple of days, Marcia and the boys had been decorating the house every afternoon and on into the evening. There were spiderwebs in the corners of the living room and dining room with big hairy spiders clinging to them. There were ghosts swishing on brooms from the beams in the library and tombstones on the front and back lawns. The pumpkins had been carved, the costumes selected. Trevor simply wanted to be a cowboy, but Kyle, with his mother's help, had decided on being a gum ball machine. He was going to wear red tights and a red sweatshirt for the stand and then a big, see-through garbage bag full of multicolored helium balloons attached to his head. Mother and son were thrilled with the idea, giggling as they'd conceived it, giggling now as she practiced attaching the headgear, the balloons jostling silently around the big, clear bag. In his chaps and fringed vest, Trevor watched intently, hand on his holster. David watched him watching. The other families were coming early, just after dark. There would be trick-or-treating and then dinner and ghost stories told around the fireplace. And then Viagra.

"David, you and Trevie light the candles," Marcia said. "Kyle and I will run up and get ready."

They disappeared up the stairs, chatting—toddler-talk, mommy-talk, exhilarated costume conspirators—while he and Trevor began lighting the candles. They were everywhere, every size and shape, huge two-foot, twisted gold ones on the floor around the fireplace and tall vanilla tapers on the tables, little orange pumpkin ones with happy and sad faces and up the front walk and all through the backyard, little paper bags of sand with votives in them. There were rules and rituals. Halloween was a candles-only night. So Marcia had mandated. He loved all that—their rituals, spinning out behind them and in front of them. He watched his son lean to light the votives, one by one, squatting down over the little bags, reaching in carefully with the long matches David handed him, each successive candle lighting up his little face under his cowboy hat.

"It's beautiful, isn't it, Daddy?" Trevor said solemnly, standing in the middle of the front hall when they came back in, all the candles flickering wildly from the wind of the front door opening and closing.

"But it's spooky, too," David said, drawing out the spooky in a scary voice.

"No, Daddy, no," Trevor said, reaching for his father's hand. "We're here together."

Kyle came crashing down the stairs, shrieking, "Look at me, look at me, I'm a red gum post, I'm a red gum post."

"Not a gum post," Trevor said. "You're the bottom of a gum ball machine."

"No, I'm a gum post," Kyle shrieked again. "Look at my face, Mommy even made my face red."

"You don't know anything," Trevor said. "You're such a baby."

"Hey, hey, stop it," Marcia said, coming down. She was dressed like a flapper, waistless, white satin dress, long rope of pearls, a silver ribbon encrusted with crystals tied around her forehead, a matching one at her neck. She shimmered in the candlelight—all glossy dark hair and bright red lipstick, which she normally never wore.

"You're so beautiful, Mommy," Trevor said, stroking the bottom of her dress.

David went upstairs to put on his costume. She whispered, smiling red lips to his ear as he passed her on the stairs: "I have nothing on underneath."

A little conjugal come-on. The image was supposed to tease him through the night as he watched her here and there, the perfect hostess and perfect mother, slithering through the guests in her white gown, crotch against satin. Instead it made him unbearably sad.

He sat on the edge of the bed, listening to his family downstairs—boys wrangling, his pantiless wife exclaiming: "Come on Kyle, hold still." The doorbell rang, he heard Mary Lou's voice, then Trevor screeching. She must be in something wild. He slipped into his own costume, carefully collected over the past couple of days. Camouflage suit, dog tags, boots and the pièces de résistance: medals. He carefully pinned them on in the mirror without catching his own eye.

They were in the living room, the two women and the two boys, Marcia and Mary Lou bent over, still trying to secure Kyle's head of balloons. Mary Lou straightened as he came in—unfurling six feet of pink flamingo, tights, wings, beak.

"Fantastic," he said. "Your best ever."

Marcia looked up sideways at him. She was kneeling, a piece of red masking tape in her hand. She stood abruptly, dropping the bag. Balloons swooshed out everywhere and Kyle burst into tears.

"Screw you," Marcia said, as she walked past him out the door. Trevor began to cry while Mary Lou folded herself into pink halves and began picking up balloons.

"Come on you guys," she said to the boys, "No more crying. We'll fix it. You," she said to David, "fix that," gesturing with her head toward the stairs.

He found Marcia lying on her side of the big white bed, dark hair fanned out against the pillow lace.

"Not funny, huh?" he said, sitting down on his side.

She didn't move or look up.

"I'm sorry," he said. "I'm trying."

"This is getting boring," she finally said. "I thought we were getting somewhere."

The doorbell started to ring serially, people piling in, exclaiming, laughing. Someone started up the stairs but stopped. "Come on you guys," Mary Lou shouted above the downstairs din. "The kids are dying to get going."

Marcia sat up, swinging her legs onto the floor.

"What do you want to do?" she said.

"Now, you mean?"

"Now, later, whenever."

Mary Lou shouted up again, but neither moved.

"Maybe we should have another baby," he said.

"Right," she said, standing abruptly and walking by him to her chest of drawers. "How the hell do you expect us to do that?" she said, pulling up a pair of underpants.

The theater of the evening absorbed both. Everyone got geared up—coats recently taken off were put back on, plastic pumpkin buckets handed around to all the kids. A couple of the fathers stayed home to watch the basketball game, hovering around the set—a surgeon in green scrubs and a skinhead with a big fake tattoo of a skeleton on his arm. The fire was lit and the food was smelling good. A house rich in good things, a house to return to. Outside, the just-dark streets were chilly and a thin film of fog covered everything in a damp fuzz—trees, houses, cars. They were out early so the other groups they passed were also made up of small children and parents, some carrying paper cups full of wine. David smelled it as they passed. Marcia, in a full-length fake silver mink, arm through Mary Lou's wing, sauntered on ahead with Trevor while David, now in black tie (he didn't know what else to switch into), dawdled with Kyle.

"Daddy," he'd say periodically with panic in his voice, lifting his pudgy hand to pat his bag of balloons, "it's going to blow away."

"No," David kept saying, "it'll be fine."

Marty, in Clinton mask, dropped back to chat. "Wanna play tomorrow?"

"I can't. It's Saturday."

"So?"

"So you know so. I don't play on the weekends."

"You trying to win husband of the year award or something?"

"I got a lock on it."

"That's not what I hear."

"Screw you," David said.

"Hey, lighten up. I was just razzing you." Marty walked off.

It might have been an innocent poke, but David didn't believe it. He took it as proof of what he'd secretly suspected. That everyone knew something. That's the way things went. Nothing was private anymore. Women told each other everything. Men, too, sometimes, younger men, but not David and not these other husbands. They were still of a generation whose fathers had told them not to talk about their business—so they didn't, even though the world had certainly changed. In David's experience it was the women who were flagrant now, unrestrained, dissective. They told each other everything and then the wives told their husbands and then the husbands needled each other in a semi-oblique way the way Marty had just done to David. A little verbal elbow to the ribs—jab, jab—trying to get at the tender places. He wondered just how graphic she'd been: his silken flapper. Her laugh floated back to him and his heart momentarily lifted. She was his wife. He loved her. She was up there at the head of the pack, leading the way in her silvery fur. It would all be OK. He would be OK. To hell with everybody who knew anything. What did it matter?

"Daddy, I'm tired," Kyle said.

David reached down to pick him up. He carried him up toward Marcia and Mary Lou. "Oh look," she said, "a maitre d' carrying a gum ball machine."

She leaned to kiss Kyle on the head. "Nice duds," she said to David.

He eyeballed her hard. She knew it all for sure—down to every last detail. The rage and betrayal bumped up against his chemically enhanced equanimity. Knock, knock, let me out. But he had his now cranky baby in his arms and the night was suburban-sweet and damp, full of excited kids and parents with paper cups of wine, and at home, there were friends and a big fire and bowls of homemade chili in three thoughtful varieties: regular, chicken, and vegetarian. Got to admit it: she was something.

"I'm going to take him back," he said, turning to go. "See you there."

"Bring me more candy," Kyle yelled back at his mom. "More candy."

"Scoot over," Mary Lou said, "you're crushing my wing." David had plopped down next to her on the sofa. She'd just been awarded first prize for the best costume, strutting on her tall pink legs before the fireplace while the kids and parents all hooted and clapped. David had been given the booby prize for least imaginative getup. He smiled and bowed and said costumes were for kids.

"Lame-o," the crowd chanted at him. Now everyone was in place for the ghost stories, candles burning down, swords and pistols, a bird beak and a surgeon's smock, and a handful of ghoulish masks in a pile on the floor behind the sofa, underneath a confetti of glittery candy wrappers. A bloodcurdling scream came from the den and then a skeleton danced into the room. The kids screamed and grabbed each other or their parents, as the skeleton launched into a spooky story about waking up underground in a grave and coming back to life, to this very house to visit these very children.

The room was dead quiet, the kids rapt. Marcia stood up after a few minutes and asked the skeleton to please leave. These were good children and they did not deserve to be haunted. Oh OK, the skeleton agreed, slithering away. A witch followed, cackling into the room.

"It's Karen," a couple of the kids screamed. "Look at her shoes."

The witch poked her long fake finger at the kids. "Shh or I'll cut your tongues out."

"Getting a little heavy this year," David whispered to Mary Lou. "We'll be up on those child abuse charges—you know, cutting up animals in front of them and making them drink the blood."

"Right," she laughed.

They sat for a while listening to the witch, then she leaned toward him. "You know," she whispered, "she'll get everything."

"What are you talking about?"

"You know damn well. Everything: the house, the kids, us," gesturing at the room full of people. "All of it. That's the way it works."

"Bullshit," he said lightly. "You women didn't want it that way anymore. It's fifty-fifty."

"Yeah, but you're too nice. You'd never make her sell."

"Jesus, isn't this a little heavy? Who's talking about anything like that?"

"I am," she said, still whispering out of the side of her mouth while both continued to watch the witch. "You're going to have to forgive her, David."

"Tonight?" he said, reaching for a little of the old glibness.

"Sooner the better," she said.

"Am I being threatened?"

"Come on, David. You know I love you. We all do."

"Sure," he said, getting up. "I'm just going to go pop my Viagra. I'll be sure to send you all an E-mail tomorrow and let you know how it worked."

Walking up the stairs, he suddenly hated all of them. They were not friends but some prurient claque. So what if she got them—and the house. He suddenly hated it, too, with all its perfect little touches: the off-white walls, the beige wool carpet, the flowers and candles and those fucking boats. It was some highly decorated family set. And he was playing a part he didn't like—or couldn't get right. Husband as patient. Or maybe it was the opposite: he was nailing the part in spite of himself.

He took off his pumps, suit, studs, turned out the lights and crawled into bed. He'd been doing his best. Going to the shrink. Taking his pills like a good boy. He heard Kyle's particular screech and his mother's loud hushing, then creepy music. Someone had put on a movie. After a while he smelled popcorn and then heard the front door opening, the first families slipping away into the foggy night. He saw them all, everyone he loved, in their silly costumes and camaraderie—far, far away down the stairs in another world where he once so happily lived. It was that child-sick feeling, the adults out there bustling about, talking about you in hushed tones, laughing, eating, carrying on, while you lay limp and feverish in your bed wondering if you'd ever be well again. At one point, the door opened. He'd heard the steps coming and feigned sleep. The door shut. He figured it was Marcia or maybe Mary Lou. Womankind coming to check the patient. Tiptoe, tiptoe. But they were his tormentors now, too. They'd put him on notice. He heard the front door open again and muffled voices on the front porch below his bedroom window. He couldn't hear what they were saying, but could

imagine it. Great night. Thanks. Hope David's OK. Everyone gracefully pretending he was lying up here with the onset of the flu or something when they knew damn well it had nothing to do with that. He
could hear them in the car on the way home, husbands and wives chatting softly so as not to wake the kids strapped in back, their candy-
sticky little faces already pitched forward in sleep. Sad what's
happening. They seemed so perfect. I doubt it's fatal. I don't know, you
never know. Jeez, I'll miss her food, the husband would say. Bastard,
the wife might say, with a mock-competitive edge, but there would be
affection in it. She would touch his thigh and he might reach down and
cover her hand because they were still intact and grateful for it, sitting
there in their costumes—pea-green surgical scrubs on him, a nurse's
hat bobby pinned to her head, stethoscope still around her neck—
children asleep in back, their gratitude turning, with every mile, into
an aphrodisiac, so that once home, kids transferred from carseats to
beds, lights out downstairs, phone machine checked, they would make
love—not raucous sex, just the easy, warm, slightly smug screwing of
two people who have just left close friends whose marriage is clearly
imperiled. David knew the scenario. He knew that sex. He and Marcia
had had it. Now they, the Sandersons, had become the sexual prompts
for the tribe. Their misfortunes (he had no doubt anymore that everyone knew everything) had stirred the lusty, Halloween-night witches
brew that had sent their friends scurrying home to copulate and cling
to each other. Oh, he knew it. He saw them, heard them, hated them.
And envied them. He switched on his reading light. He had the bedside table now of an old man: all those little amber pill bottles with
their childproof safety caps. Pain pills, potency pills, mood pills, sleeping pills. What should it be? He hesitated, then reached for the Viagra.
Should he? It was late. But what a nice surprise, hey? They could make
that new baby this very night. A little girl, a beautiful dark-haired little
girl. He popped one in his mouth, rolling the little blue diamond-

shaped tablet around on his tongue. A miracle, it was, such a pill, a gift from the chemical gods. Men throughout history would no doubt have sold their souls for such a gift. Caesar and Napoleon, men in tights and men in togas, men in breeches and kilts and cummerbunds—all lusting for that extra kick that he, David Sanderson, had lolling around his mouth at this very moment. Virility restored. But what if it didn't work? And what if Trevor had one of his nightmares and called out. Wasn't there something corny or obscene about taking it with kids asleep in the other room? And what if his wife came to bed still angry and didn't want anything to do with him—he with his big, shiny, optimistic hard-on? He couldn't bear the rejection. The scenarios spun though his mind, lickety split, and back again and, reaching for the light, he spit the pill out in his hand before it had a chance to completely dissolve. His heart was pounding. He got up to get a glass of water, kicking through his fallen soldier suit on the hall floor, cutting his baby toe on one of the sharp medals. He cursed and hopped into the bathroom so as not to drip blood on the carpet. He washed his small wound and put on a Band-Aid, one of those child ones with a purple dinosaur on it because he couldn't find the adult size. What a joke he was. They were right: he was a lame-o. Big time. Sliding back under the covers, he reached for the sleeping pills and took two before he could reconsider.

"So what's taking so long?" Dr. Lou said. He said it with practiced joviality, that telegenic twinkle with just a hint of an R-rated leer embedded in it. It was in response to David's admission that while, yes, he had filled his prescription for Viagra, he had yet to try it.

"The usual," Marcia said. "Too much work, too little time."

David looked at her. She was covering for him. His heart stirred a little. It was—for a moment again—them against the world. He smiled at her. She caught it.

"What?" she said, hopefully.

"Nothing."

"Come on, David," Lou said.

"He's been pretty down again," Marcia said.

"David?"

"Maybe it's the Prozac," Marcia said. "Maybe it's not working."

"No, the recovery process just takes some time."

Ah recovery. That's what he was in. Everybody was in it. Everybody in the whole, wide, fucking country. Getting over drugs or food or childhood abuse. He was just trying to recover from having been happily married.

"We've found that it takes longer for men to get over adultery than for women."

"Really?" Marcia said. She was interested. Next thing, she'd be writing an article on it.

"Sounds sexist to me," David said, sticking a toe back in the game.

"Yeah?" Lou said.

"The old stereotypes about women being more forgiving and men more possessive."

"You think it's wrong?" Lou said.

"Let's bring your wife in and ask her."

"David," Marcia said sharply.

"We can do that," Lou said without, as always, registering a dart or missing a beat. "You can ask her yourself. Might be helpful in fact. Helen actually runs a forgiveness group. You might want to try it. They meet Thursday nights at that big Presbyterian Church up on Mulholland."

"A forgiveness group," David said, half under his breath, realizing just how deep he—a rational, respectable, middle-aged, mortgage-paying agnostic—had stumbled into the surreal world of self-help. It was like falling into a vat of Jell-O. He wasn't sure how to get out.

Baloop, baloop—he was swimming toward the side but couldn't touch it. He appealed to his wife, looking at her. They were going to drown here in this stuff, didn't she see? It was time to try something different.

"It's time to try something different," Lou said, echoing David's precise sentiment. "Look, David, we can switch your antidepressants if you want. But I don't think that's the issue. What you really need is some quality time in the sack. That's where the real . . ."

"Healing begins," Marcia said, turning to her husband with a triumphant—and complicitous—smile.

"Bingo," he said half-heartedly.

A date. That's how she couched it. A weekend date. The kids at her parents. All bets off 'til then. Take the pressure off. He watched her: she was all lit up with the enterprise of seduction. For days, the house bubbled with her energy. He left it in the morning and came back to it at night. Arrangements being made, secret phone calls, the credit card number given over the phone. Things were being planned, ordered. Caviar, foie gras, lingerie, sex toys. Who knew? The highly respectable women's magazines his wife wrote for routinely suggested gimmicks and gadgetry. He imagined everything from a stripper to a string quartet, depending on where she wanted to put the emphasis: groin or heart. He was trying to calibrate her calibration. What would work best here to revive her husband: pornography or romance? Why not both: why not a naked string quartet? He was sure that somewhere in this sprawling, raunchy city such a titillating hybrid was for hire, statuesque Julliard dropouts whose Hollywood dreams had gone bust and were now reduced to straddling their Strads and performing concertos cum fellatio. If you went down this road, there was no end of things you could think up, no end of sexual blandishments, punishments, permutations you could find or purchase. He knew about them, of course. You couldn't help hearing or reading about them. Some of his male clients had insisted on telling him about their X-rated escapades. Girls who would do this and that—in twosomes, threesomes, fivesomes. Cocaine smeared here and there. He had just never been interested. It had never been part of their marital vocabulary, their marital need. He thought of himself as a licentious square, game for intramarital explicitness, no props needed except love. Some days—particularly hot summer afternoons—when he looked from his corner office tower out over the city, he imagined the complicated and punishing pleasures underway at that very moment, as he gazed down, over there in the gated mansions of Bel Air, down there in squalid apartments in Pico Rivera, and felt again—casting his eye back toward the environs of his own house—the contentment that was his. That was yesterday. Now something weird was afoot, some kittenish alien was in his house making giggly, secretive phone calls ordering up God knows what. Coming upon her, slightly flushed, whispering into the phone, strands of her hair falling over the mouthpiece, he was stabbed by tenderness for her, the contortions she was going through—his normally self-possessed, profoundly unkittenish wife. He wanted to stop her from all this, but he couldn't. The spectacle was awful and mesmerizing. And as he reached to say, sweetheart, don't, you don't need to do this, everything will be fine in a little while—a few more Prozacs down the hatch—a wicked sense of despairing pleasure overcame him, trumping his tenderness. Fuck her. Let her turn herself into a pornographic pretzel if that's what she wanted. She'd already done that in the backseat of that car.

The boys picked up the party atmosphere. They gamboled about, trying to help, get in on the action. Marcia always let them do something for the parties—lick bowls, light candles, make cookies. This was no different. It was just like Halloween and all the holidays and party days past. She found them tasks. She didn't tell them the truth, of course, not that they would have understood. She just said she was planning a special night for Daddy because he was the best Daddy in the whole wide world. They clapped and shrieked. Their Daddy. They'd help: cut out paper hearts to tack up, make chocolates from scratch, the ones with the gooey, orangey insides he loved so much. He came home to find the three wrist deep in chocolate, smears on their foreheads and cheeks, his little boys unwitting soldiers conscripted into the campaign to woo their daddy and raise his dick.

"Daddy, look what we're making you," Trevor said, raising his chocolate-covered hands in the air.

"It's s'pose to be a s'prise," Kyle said in his loud baby voice.

"No, it's OK," Marcia said. "Daddy knows."

She looked up and smiled. It was the happy mother not the kitten. The best mother in the whole wide world. He went to kiss his boys, gently licking the chocolate off one forehead and then the other. "Don't I get one?" Marcia said. The kitten was back. He kissed her lightly on the forehead and went to pour himself a big double Scotch, wondering how all this was going to end.

Thursday night. One night to go before the big date. Marcia was taking the boys to an afternoon movie and early dinner with Gwen and her two kids. David stayed at his desk past seven, peering at numbers on the computer screen 'til his eyes got tired and the numbers started gyrating on the screen. Time for glasses? Imminent, he thought. He got in his Jeep and headed toward home, realizing halfway there that there was no way they'd be home yet and that he couldn't stand being alone. Normally he loved it, arriving home, the house so quiet while he changed into his sweats, turned on the news, poured a glass of wine, all the time waiting pleasurably in the silence for the car to pull in, the doors to slam, the family babble to reach his ears and then the door opening, the boys immediately and noisily looking for him—Trevor always, sometimes Kyle, sometimes both. Then Marcia would come in, looking frazzled, but no less lovely—

more so to him sometimes in her maternal frazzlement, a little less crisp, more fatigued and needy—and plop down beside him. He'd get her a glass of wine and they'd talk and he'd rub her feet while the boys had their last hurrah of playing, a last few cartoons on the VCR, until Marcia, with her unerring instinct to call a halt before the boys fell into tears or brawls, nodded at David and he got up to do the night-time ritual. Baths, teeth, stories. Now he didn't want to be there waiting alone, tempted to drink too much, feel too maudlin, all those beckoning pills on his bedside table. Maybe she was right. Maybe the Prozac wasn't working anymore. Maybe he'd had all the kick he was going to get. It was as if his despair was leaking around the edges of the antidepressant. He feared the chemical dike was about to give— and then what? His wife, he had clearly been warned, was running out of patience. Which is how he found himself parked up on Mulholland across from the big, architecturally blah but effortful stone and glass church in whose basement the regular Thursday-night forgiveness meeting was about to begin. It was clear and cold out, the entire city basin windswept and twinkly, lights visible on distant mountains and along the coast, a sliver of a moon. He sat in his car, motor running, heater on, watching people arrive, a few hanging outside to have a last smoke, moving antsily to keep warm. Were these the forgivers or the forgivees? Did they come together to give and receive the mea culpas? He didn't know the protocol. Was he really going to go in here? If there was a crowd, maybe. He'd been, as he always did with everything, unconsciously counting. There were at least twenty-three people in there by now, give or take. He could slip in the back and stay hidden. Mrs. Lou had never seen him so she'd have no reason to recognize him. He looked at his watch—almost eight, starting time. He could wait another few minutes, then sneak in. After eight, he'd be noticed. It was now or never. A couple more cars came and he made ready to join the last participants, trail in anonymously behind them.

Out of the car, a last nod at the moon and the shimmering city below, then off to the basement of God's house to listen to the tales of betrayal and redemption. Was it really possible that he was here, he, David Sanderson? Just one more step down—or was it up—the slippery self-help slope. He hesitated on the stairs going down, but something propelled him on, some mixture of voyeurism and desperation.

He slipped into the room without looking around, suddenly fearful that someone would recognize him. He was in a folding chair on the back left-hand side, Mrs. Lou—Helen—speaking invitingly in her well-modulated voice (of course, she, too, had one of those pleasingly deep, soothy-soothy TV voices), welcoming the "old-timers and our newcomers," before he dared look up and look around. The room was full, a three-chair deep semi-circle of the mostly well-dressed, women in turtlenecks and pants, modified makeup, men in suits or postwork jogging clothes. He had carefully changed out of his suit jacket into a sweater he kept in the car so as not to ID himself as too preppy and elitist, but that precaution was unnecessary. He should have known. Forgiveness was—as he had learned—a costly business.

Helen was recognizable from TV and from the photograph in her husband's office, though looking, in person, even more the elegant senior with blondish gray hair pulled into a decorous knot at the nape of her neck, restrained makeup highlighting her cheekbones and blue, blue eyes. She, too, wore a dark, plum-colored turtleneck and matching slacks, delicate (undoubtedly expensive) jewelry—the uniform clearly for the female attendees. His wife would fit right in.

"All right," she said, "anyone contemplate homicide or suicide this week? Come on," she said, with a broad, eye-crinkling smile. "No hands?"

She got her titter. The group immediately started to thaw, look around at each other, share knowing nods and smiles. She had her husband's touch, maybe learned from him. David figured her to be the patrician yin to her husband's burly, streetwise yang. Yet she too had gone public, long since overcoming whatever well-bred inhibitions she once might have had. Maybe she liked all that New Age gutter-speak about quality sack time. Maybe it was a turn on.

A slightly plump female volunteer with a head of black curls then read the mission statement. "We in the forgiveness group do not come to judge each other. We will listen with open hearts and minds to our own loved ones as well as to others. We will not criticize or interrupt. We are here to be supportive. We know that we are not perfect and that forgiveness is hard work. It is the conscious effort to move past betrayal and let go of wounds and resentments. That is our purpose."

"Thanks, Marlene," everyone seemed to say in unison. A man sitting next to her patted her on the back when she sat down. Was he her betrayer or vice versa?

A couple was introduced, a mother and her grown son, Connie and Lake. Clearly some family name. They were a handsome pair, tall, dark hair, dark eyes, pale skin. David figured Connie to be maybe fifty, Lake twenty-four or twenty-five. They held hands as they moved to the front of the group, taking their place beside Helen—or Mrs. Lou, as David preferred.

The woman spoke first. She seemed self-assured, but as her narrative progressed, she began mumbling. Mrs. Lou moved to put an arm around her and the son picked up the story. They had worked hard, he said, to forgive his dad, who had had an affair with his secretary. The son had seen him with her in a restaurant and later confronted him. He had confessed all to his wife and begged for forgiveness. He promised he would never see her again. They all wept—mother, father, son. That was five years ago. Two years ago, he was killed in the crash of a private plane. The secretary went down with him. Since then, the mother and son had struggled with their feelings of anger and resentment. The group had helped a lot.

They sat down. People clapped and kept turning to look at them, some with tears in their eyes. David joined the clapping so as not to draw attention to himself.

"I think we can agree that Connie and Lake are an inspiration to us all in their fight to forgive," Mrs. Lou said. "I know many of you have heard me say this, but I just want to leave it with you before the break. Resentment is like acid. It eats the container. See you back in your seats in ten minutes."

David fled into the bathroom so as not to be swept up in the forgiveness family, cohering, as he left, around Connie and Lake. He felt as if he'd tumbled into one of those daytime talk shows. He and Marcia had watched them intently during the time she was prone, trying to fight off the premature labor contractions with Kyle, laughing at the poor slobs who were willing to mortify themselves for their few paltry minutes in the limelight. Sure, the dress and diction might be better here, but wasn't the impulse the same?

David was intending to leave but as he came out of the bathroom he ran right into Mrs. Lou, who was coming out of the adjacent women's restroom. She looked, he thought, even better up close.

"This is your first time, isn't it?" she said. "I'm Helen."

"David," he said looking down, trying to duck under her radiantly conscriptive and sympathetic smile.

"How did you find us?"

"I looked under forgiveness in the phone book," he said.

She stood there with her unswerving smile. He felt a bit chagrined. "I'm—that is, my wife and I—are seeing your husband."

"It's not easy," she said, now reaching to touch his arm. "I know, I've been there."

"Yeah," he said churlishly, irritated that she had instantly intuited he—like her—was the wronged party, "the whole fucking world knows that."

Not a wince. She was just like her husband. You couldn't rile them. She tightened her grip on his arm, smiling eyes still on him. "Coming back in?" she said.

He followed her like an obedient child and took his seat. A couple in slippery exercise suits (David tried to read the fine print of the logo on her chest but couldn't) was already sitting facing each other on the small stage. They looked to be in their early forties—he graying at the temples, she with an artfully messy reddish shag that she kept fluffing up with her hands. Helen introduced them as Molly and Peter and said they were this week's couple for the "forgiveness ceremony." Everyone settled into attention. Helen sat down. Molly, tearing up, took one hand out of her hair and reached, with it, to take her husband's hand.

"I, Molly, love you, Peter," she said in a low voice. "I am sorry I hurt you. You did not deserve it. If you open your heart to me, I will never betray your trust again."

David wondered: was it the personal trainer, the yoga instructor, the contractor? The audience's attention had already turned to Peter. Presumably it was now his turn to recite his more or less prescripted bit: I, Peter, forgive you, Molly . . . Instead his jaw quivered. He could not speak. The audience hung on his silence. David, too, was suddenly riveted. Would he erupt, castigate the bitch, and flee from the room? How many there secretly hoped so? David looked around and then back at Peter, silently sending him encouraging messages. Wouldn't somebody stand up for heartbreak, not be cajoled out of their rage and grief? David imagined running after him, putting an arm around him, the two of them going off somewhere to get bitterly and commiseratively drunk together.

Peter started to say something, but then fell silent again. The group was rapt. Was this unusual, this hesitation? David didn't know, but it seemed so. There wasn't a squeak, a chair shuffle, a coffee cup being picked up or down. Peter started again and stopped. Helen kept her place. David's heart was pounding. Go for it man, go for it, his inner voice said.

Molly look concerned. She made a gesture of encouragement with her head. Peter looked at her. Finally he started again. "I've always loved you but . . ." He stopped again. No one moved. David silently implored him not to give in, not to capitulate. He was the hope of humankind, sitting there, Gary Cooper, the lonesome holdout against the whole audience, the whole town, the whole world, the whole wide modern world, the pap-spouting, Prozac-prescribing fixers and schmoozers who would take the ragged sorrows of a man's heart and turn them into mawkish pabulum to be served up for public consumption. Pain was not a spectator sport. And Peter here was the holdout, the one person in the whole misbegotten basement-slash-world that seemed to get it, that seemed, with his hesitation, to be on the brink of taking the last grand stand. Oh yes, yes Peter, do it for all of us. We're out here, your comrades in grief. We're here and we're rooting for you. Don't do it, Peter. Don't throw in the towel. Don't forgive her. Not here. Not now. Stand tall on the ceremony of your wounds. You could be a hero, after all, in this world. You might not get medals for bravery in battle. But we, your fellow sufferers, we will applaud you and bandy about your name with reverence. Do it for all of us, Peter. Do it for me.

Helen twitched in her seat. The audience twitched back. Peter looked out at them. He looked back at his wife. "I . . . I've loved you since . . ." It was good, promising. He would speak of her loveliness, her perfidiousness, the cruel juxtaposition of the two. He would take back the narrative for all of them, restore their poetic dignity. No mealy-mouthed, teary-eyed, cliché-ridden crumbs for the audience. Oh no. Peter would do it. He would do it.

"I'm sorry," he said, looking at the audience again, raising David's hopes even more. "I'm a little nervous. I love my wife . . ."

"Peter, tell her," Helen said softly.

Suddenly his voice was stronger. "I, Peter, love you, Molly . . ." David held his breath . . . "and I am struggling on the path of forgiveness."

164 · ANNE TAYLOR FLEMING

"Oh, shit," David said, much louder than he meant to. The entire group turned and stared. He saw the flare of anger before they had a chance to tuck it back under their insistent empathy. You don't get it yet, their collective look said. No problem. We'll be here for you when you do. It was he who bolted from the room.

What jackasses, he repeated, as he climbed the stairs, crossed the street, acknowledged the moon, unlocked the car. But by the time he sat, his smug elation had transmuted into a ferocious longing. Where did he belong anymore? Where? He had been exiled from his happiness. And he certainly didn't belong here—in this overheated basement of tony atoners. He sat looking out over the vast, sparkling city, feeling lost, homeless, the way new arrivals often said they felt here: unmoored, overwhelmed. That was why, he suspected, they found their way to all these groups, hundreds meeting out there now, repenters of all stripes—drinkers and eaters and child abusers—offering up confessions in church basements and community centers, eliciting the benediction of their fellow miscreants and self-appointed gurus. He heard the confessional chorus rising up from the city floor, floating up up up, thousands of voices, an a cappella crescendo of atonement and absolution. He was supposed to join, throw his own small voice into the mix. They were after him. They were all after him to give it up, forgive and get on with it. He covered his ears and put his head down on the steering wheel. Was he finally really losing it? Was the Prozac making him crazy? He suddenly started to laugh at the memory of swearing at Mrs. Lou. He never said things like that—the whole fucking world knows. Never. But the chorus picked up and drowned out the giggles. We're sorry, we're sorry, you're forgiven, you're forgiven, hallelujah, hallelujah—swoops of contrapuntal voices. He squeezed his palms tighter against his ears. There was a gentle knock on the window. He looked up into Mrs. Lou's blue, blue eyes. No way he was going to roll down the window. He gave her a thumbs-up and a big, fake smile and turned the key in the ignition. She backed away from the car and he drove off. About a half a block from his house he slid to a stop at the curb and turned the motor off. Their bedroom light was still on and he didn't want to face Marcia or certainly tell her where he'd been. If he told her, she'd be momentarily too tickled for his taste and then despairing at his undisguisable contempt. Fifteen minutes later the light went off. He quietly let himself into the house and went to have his now customary double neat Scotch. When it took the edge off his memory of the evening, he climbed the stairs in stocking feet. There was an envelope taped to their bedroom door. He took it and went into the guest bathroom to read it. "My Dearest David. I can't wait for tomorrow. Why don't we spend the night apart like the night before our wedding. Remember? I love you. M."

When he got home the next afternoon, Marcia's mother was there in the driveway picking up the kids. They were already strapped in. He pressed his face against the side windows of the car, one and then the other, to make them giggle. Neither he nor Marcia's still-attractive mother looked directly at each other. She routinely came to get the kids. It was no big deal, but he didn't want to know she knew this was a big deal. He watched them drive off, small hands waving frantically, little voices just audible through the slightly cracked windows: Bye Daddy. Bye. His heart scrambled after the car. Don't leave me. Don't leave me here alone.

He stood there for a long time after the car had turned the corner. It was a gloomy day, darkening fast. There were no kids on the street. There were never any kids on the streets anymore, not in these suburbs. They all had too many expensive inside toys, too many nervous parents. David and his friends had played hard through many cold, Eastern winter afternoons, tossing balls in the street, inventing games, sometimes going back out after dinner. He saw them there in the street whooping and hollering. Now those boys had become fear-filled fathers. Things change. He felt eyes on him from somewhere in the house, but turning saw no one. He needed to go in.

He entered quietly as was his new habit, no banging down of a briefcase, no "I'm home." He looked around. The house was like a woman all dressed up for seduction. Low lights, flowers everywhere, big yellow bunches of them, and good smells drifting from the kitchen. On the front hall mirror was another envelope. "David—#2," it said on it. It was to be an adult treasure hunt apparently. OK. He would play along. He reached for it, hoping—well, what did he hope?—that she hadn't penned some provocative note. It would be a false move and he figured her to be too smart for that. She wouldn't make that mistake. Not his wife. He pulled it off the mirror and opened it. It was an invitation to dinner in front of the fireplace with a fancy printed menu attached. Early on in their romance, when they were giddy about sharing their pleasures, they would do this: tease each other with invitations and menus. He would call home and say he was stopping for caviar and champagne. She would fax him that night's dinner menu to work. Just then, he heard her come in the back door, but her note forbade him to find her. He was to climb the stairs and have a hot bath. He would find it already drawn. She had timed it, but how? Calling Mindy or getting Mindy to call her—everyone in on the canard, the reclamation scheme. He'd have to stop those thoughts if he were going to get through this. He mounted the stairs, reading the menu. Each course had an accompanying wine selection, from Napa or Bordeaux. There were asterisks, in varying numbers from one to four, after each wine selection and down below, corresponding explanations of the date of each wine: the year we met, the year we married, the year Trevor was born, the year Kyle was born. She had gone all out: it was Marcia at her seductively sentimental best. He loosened himself toward it. She was doing her part. He would have to do his. He would be a good sport. He would yield to her wifely ministrations.

In the bedroom were two presents and his black-tie suit—all cleaned from Halloween—laid out on the bed. One present had the #3 note. He opened it. Inside were two little hearts from the boys taped to a navy blue terry cloth robe. He stripped and put it on and headed toward the bathroom when his eye caught the #4 note taped to a flute of champagne on top of the dresser. He heard a car pull up, a couple of doors close, then someone—or was it a couple of some-ones—coming up the walk. Caterers, strippers, the support staff for his seduction? He was able to smile. He should try to have some fun with this, no? He swilled the champagne, half a flute, and headed for the bathroom. Peekaboo—any notes here? Indeed: #5 was taped to the mirror. Brenda, the masseuse, would be up at 6:15. He took another sip of champagne and got into the bath. We're having fun now. Brenda will be up forthwith—our fair-haired, firm-handed Brenda. She will anoint us with oil. She will knead our shoulders and calves, a strand of her long hair sometimes escaping its blonde braid and tickling across our exposed rump. Yes, yes, yum, yum. And yet, this night, as on previous nights, lying face down on her heated table, head in that silly, awkward doughnut, it will not be her, never be her he fantasizes about. Or any of the rest of them. It is his wife he wants. Wants to want. Wants to want to want. Has wanted. Will want again. With a little help from our friend over there on the nightstand. This is it, folks, D-day, date night for the Sandersons of Loring Avenue. Stay tuned.

After his massage, he had a shower, washing off the oil. Eucalyp-tus—was that it, that pungent, piney smell? It was time for present #6. He opened it. Silken royal blue underpants. Not for her—which he first thought. But for him. This for a man who had never worn any-thing racier than cotton boxer shorts in white and blue—the occa-sional holiday pair stamped with Santa Clauses, courtesy of the boys. Maybe he should put those on instead. Maybe he should call this whole thing off now, put the robe back on, march downstairs and say calmly, there's been a mistake here, I don't think I can do this. I can't wear these things. He sat down on the edge of the bed, silk briefs in hand, listening to the hum of downstairs preparations. Finally he reached for the phone and dialed Marcia's mother.

"Hey Aileen, it's me. Everything fine? . . . Great. Let me talk to Trevor or whichever one's closest . . . Hey baby, it's Daddy . . . I love my robe . . . You did . . . You've helped Grammie make up the bed . . . Good boys . . . Hey punkie, I love my robe . . . Yeah, Daddy misses you too . . . OK, let me talk to Grammie . . . Yeah, OK, we'll call at bedtime."

He sat there immobile 'til there was a soft knock on the door.

"David, it's me. Are you about ready?" He didn't answer. Maybe she'd come in. Maybe she'd see. Still life: nude contemplating royal blue jockey shorts. She'd get it. She'd see him sitting there and she'd see. She'd call it off. But she didn't come in.

"Everything's ready," she said. "I can't wait for you to see."

The old Marcia. His wife. His enthusiastic wife, proudly dragging him around the house to show him this or that flower arrangement or new fabric or re-framed family photograph. Or into the kitchen to sample a new dish before the guests came. That's what this was, a variation on a theme. All he had to do was relax and play along. And take his pills. It was now or never. He reached over and picked up the bottle. He emptied a couple into his hand. He was supposed to take only one the first time out. He put one in the back of this throat and tipped up his head, washing it down with the last sip of lukewarm champagne. Why not: Viagra and champagne, the perfect date-night combo. Then, on an impulse, he decided to bite off another half and throw it after the first. Two might be asking for trouble, but another half, why not? A booster. Nobody died of this shit, except old men with bad hearts. He was just a relatively young man with a broken one. For him, the doctors assured, Viagra was the savior not the killer.

All right. All systems go. He had signed on and he would see it through.

He slipped on the silk panties, shimmying them up his legs. He had a visceral intimation of femininity, silky things against skin. It was not unpleasant, just weird. He tucked his genitals into their slick new home then put on his penguin suit—pleated shirt, bow tie, studs, slipped on his black patent pumps and then again came to a halt on the edge of the bed. He reached for the phone and started dialing Marcia's mother but he put it down before it rang. He would try to let them recede, those two small faces, and let float instead onto his mental video screen the no-doubt silken-swathed private parts of their mom. Would she also be in royal blue—a sign of their sartorial solidarity? Mr. and Mrs. Sanderson in the His and Her Underwear Line from Calvin Klein.

He walked slowly down the stairs. Floated really. He had that same otherworldly, hallucinatory feeling he'd been having lately. Marcia was not in the living room when he entered. It was, he had to admit, magical. A roaring fire. The yellow bouquets. Yellow tapers on the damask covered round table in front of the fireplace. A new female jazz singer he couldn't place crooning in the background. Fantasyland for an intimate dinner à deux. Right out of some trendy lifestyle magazine. The champagne bottle was jauntily atilt in a standing silver bowl. Clearly one of the new purchases. He took one of the seats and decided to have some more champagne. What did it matter at this point to throw a little more alcohol into the chemical stew? Nobody had said you couldn't swill with the pills. He figured Marcia had asked and would monitor the situation. He noticed then an envelope on the plate in front of him: #7. Dun da dun da. He read: "Dear David: I hope after tonight we can be close again." Just then, Marcia entered, carrying something on a small plate. She was in a long, deep blue gown, strapless, and had cut her dark hair to her chin, with thick, straight bangs. She did look stunning, like that old movie star Louise something—he couldn't remember her name. He stood as she came.

"OK?" she smiled, setting down little potato skins full of caviar. "Nobody will bother us. They'll do the stuff out there, but I'll get it."

"You look beautiful," he said.

"You really like it?" she said, touching her hair. "It feels so different."

"It's very dramatic," he said, "but you can pull it off."

"Have one," she said, pointing at the potato skins. "I had it sent from that place in New York. You 'member the one we went to on Madison."

They'd eaten it there with nothing but spoons—no toast, no blinis, no crème fraiche, no nothing. Spoons.

"We ate it with spoons," he said.

She smiled.

"We're flirting," he said.

"To us," she said, "lifting her flute."

"To us," he said. "Thanks for the note—notes." This was going to be good. This was going to be sweet. This was going to be fine.

"There're more," she said with a flick of a leer. She'd gone feline on him again, peering out from these sultry new bangs, Dr. Lou's handmaiden. David felt as if he had once more lost his footing. But then Marcia resurfaced.

"Ready for the next course?"

She came back with soup bowls, a clear broth with chunks of pinky-white lobster, just as the songstress launched into "My Funny Valentine." Time for the white wine, present #8, bearing the date of their first meeting: 1988. She swished in and out, but he couldn't hear the swish of her long dress, that sound he loved. He realized he'd been drinking fast. Better slow up. He stole a peek at his watch as she filled his glass. A half hour in. Approximately another hour to go 'til—presumably—blast off. This was timetable erotics. He had no idea what he felt about that now that they were actually in countdown mode. For that matter, he had no idea what he felt. He closed his eyes and tried to imagine his old wife, the efficient non-kitten in her white cotton panties. He thought of telling her, asking her: please go put those on. That's my best shot here. But he didn't want to hurt her. That might derail everything. This was her script. She had no doubt read at least some of the "How to Reinflame Your Husband," articles in those magazines she wrote for (maybe this whole treasure-hunt scheme had been laid out chapter and verse; he didn't want to think about that) and was now also into the recovery lit, so maybe she knew something he didn't know. All this must work on somebody, he thought, a lot of somebodies. Why not on me?

"What do you think?" she said.

"It's wonderful," he said. "Maybe a little parsley next time."

"Not the soup," she said.

"What?"

"The Viagra. You think it's going to work?"

"I don't know," he said. "Why not?"

"Are you feeling anything?"

"A little early," he said as jauntily as he could.

She left to get the next course.

He sat staring at the fire.

"David, are you all right?" Marcia said, setting down a plate of thin, rare meat. "You look so flushed." She put her hand on his forehead.

"I think it's the stuff."

"That's right. He did say that, didn't he, that you'd probably get flushed."

"Yeah, I guess it's a good sign—exaggerated blood flow to the extremities," he said, imitating Dr. Lou's TV sonority.

"I know he's pretty cornball," Marcia said, sitting down. "But if we hadn't gotten to him, we'd have been in real trouble."

He looked at her. Not a trace of irony.

"Should I tell them to put in the soufflés? They take about thirty-five minutes. Your favorite—the Grand Marnier."

He was touched again. Her efficient thoughtfulness. He was getting more and more flushed. Tingles in the fingers and toes and . . . and . . . could it be . . . yes, a tingle there. Praise the Lord. Praise the shrink. Praise the pill pushers. Quality time in the sack. If his cock did the leading, maybe his heart would follow. That's what they were all hoping for, wasn't it? That's what he was hoping for. Clearly she was, too, royal blue skivvies and all. I'll show you mine, if you show me yours. Who cared about decorously erotic white cotton briefs when a vibrant blue ass-slashing thong no doubt loomed? He put his hand across the table and took hers and with his other had a lovely long swallow of present #9—a glorious French Bordeaux.

"Let's bag the soufflé," he said.

They sat for a while holding hands. The songstress crooned, the fire crackled, they sipped their wine. He was, he realized, more than a little sloshed.

"I love you," he said. "I never loved anyone else."

"I know," she said.

She left the table and went into the kitchen. He heard low-decibel chatter. It went on for a few minutes and then he heard the back door open and close. Support staff all gone. Time to face the music and dance.

He went ahead upstairs and started undressing. He laughed when he got to the underwear. David Sanderson, numbers cruncher to the stars, in silk panties. And sprouting beneath them, oh yes, a full-tilt bonafide erection. The decorum here was no doubt: leave them on and let the missus slip slide them away. He got the candle from the bathroom and put it beside the bed. He lit it, turned off all the lights, and lay down on top of the comforter. A momentary shard of sobriety stabbed through his lust, carrying memories of his temptress's treachery, but he was able to smother it with sexual anticipation. She would come to him and make him whole again. He closed his eyes and waited.

She was there, warm breath on his crotch, fluttery exhalation against silk. He reached for her head, both hands. He sensed something: she wanted to be used. He wanted to use her. That's what he sensed. He pushed her head down harder. She bridled, pulled away, rolling off of him. Only then did he open his eyes.

"I'm sorry," he said.

"What for?" she said.

She was on her stomach, face turned away from him. Was this part of the new choreography? He felt awkward, lonesome, stupid.

"What's wrong?" he said.

"Nothing's wrong," she said. "Let's just keep going."

She rolled to face him. He looked down. She was indeed wearing royal blue—not a thong exactly. No, one of those crotchless jobs, lacy sides, no center. She caught his look.

"What?" she said.

"Is that what this all was—just a ploy so you could switch underwear?"

"Come on, David, not now," she said, beginning to tug at his underwear.

"Aren't you supposed to do that with your teeth?" he said, aiming for levity.

"Where'd you hear that?" she said. But she was—thankfully—smiling.

"In one of your magazines," he said, lying back.

"Which one," she said, kneeling over him, tugging his briefs off with her teeth. It was fun. They were laughing. Happily cavorting married lovers.

"OK," she said. "No hands. Agreed?"

She flipped her body around and straddled his face, leaning to take his penis in her mouth.

"Wait," he said, lifting her head after a few minutes. "I don't want to come yet."

She leaned up, arching hard down against his mouth, until she came, hands pressing heavily against his thighs. She lay down beside him. She gently cupped his balls while he stroked her head. He thought: we're home. Are we home?

"Don't do it again," he said finally.

"Is that a threat?" she said.

"No. Maybe. I don't know. I don't want to go through this again. I can't."

"So it is a threat."

"Can't you just say it: that you won't do it again."

"I didn't plan it. And I'm certainly not planning ever to do it again. OK?"

"Not really," he said, abruptly getting up. He went downstairs to find the wine. He sat in his chair at the table, staring into the embers of the fire. After a while, she came quietly up behind him, a kitten on the prowl.

"I didn't mean to upset you," she said. "Look?" She twirled in front of him in her old Swiss whites—teddy and panties.

"Come on, David. I'm not going to do it again. Here. Here's the last present—the big number ten."

He said nothing.

She sat down in his lap, nipples visible beneath the cotton.

"Come on," she said. "We were doing so well. We don't want to waste this," she said, squiggling her bottom around on his half-erect penis.

"Stop it," he said.

She got up and went into the kitchen. He could hear her cleaning, pots banging, refrigerator door opening, little Ms. Efficiency. His little white clad come bunny.

He drank a couple of quick glasses of wine, remembering he'd forgotten to call the boys and say good night. Nighty night little ones. Daddy's coming. Daddy's not coming. Ha ha. He reached for the present, rattling it. Oh yes, the missing ingredient. He opened it and voila, the sex toy: the big pink battery-operated dildo taped atop an X-rated video with one of those porno-camp titles: *The Dixie Sluts Eat Out.*

"Dear," he shouted, "look what I have for you?"

Marcia poked her head out of the kitchen. "Looky what I have," he said, brandishing the dildo in the air. "Come and impale yourself. Come and let me ram it up your moist little cunt."

She walked into the room, a look of alarm beginning to cloud her face. He felt slightly crazy. His erection was back.

"Look: two for the price of one," he said, turning on the dildo. "Take your pick."

"David," she said, "calm down."

Finally, he thought. Finally she's rattled. It spurred him on. He reached down and began stroking his cock, slowly, up and down, up and down, while staring at her. She didn't move, not a twitch. He stroked harder and then stuck the dildo in his mouth, sucking loudly as he moved it in and out. She was frozen in place. Her alarm turned to horror—a look he had never seen on her face and which, later, he would both try to forget and try to remember. He held her gaze and continued stroking himself, on and on, with the dildo, too, in and out of his mouth, in and out, in and out until, closing his eyes finally, he came with a deep guttural groan.

He opened his eyes. She had not moved. She didn't move now. Points to David Sanderson—triumphant at last.

"Here," he said, dildo outstretched as he rose to leave the room. "The passing of the baton." When she didn't take it, he dropped it at her feet.

He walked out of the room and up the stairs. He sat on the edge of the bed and looked at his pharmacopeia, cornucopia of pharmacopeia. What shall we take now? He reached for the sleeping pills.

Then, with an inebriated sweep, he leveled the dressing table, lamp, water glass, pill bottles. When Marcia came, he was on the floor, emptying the bottles over his head, a naked man amid a confetti of pills. She stood in the doorway.

"Come play," he said, scooping handfuls up from the carpet and letting them rain down over his head and body. "It's fun."

"David," she said.

"Here," he said, holding out a palm of pills, "one for you and one for me." He made a licking motion toward his hand, but just then she screamed.

"No. Don't."

He looked at her. He let his hand fall. She didn't move toward him.

"Oh shit," she said. "I left the water running downstairs." But she made no move to leave.

She stood. He sat. Finally she just sat down where she was. He closed his eyes and breathed deeply. They sat for a long time, nobody saying anything. Finally he opened his eyes and started scooping the pills up into one hand. She made a motion toward him. He looked at her and she sat back down. He got up the remaining pills and went into the bathroom. He was still pretty high. He avoided his own gaze in the mirror and opened the toilet lid. "All gone," he said to himself, dumping the pills in. "All all gone."

He got the washrag from the tub and sat down on the toilet. He let the water run until it was as cold as it was going to get, then ran the rag under it. He rung it out and held it against his forehead. He did it over and over, pressing it alternately on the back of his neck. Once, when he thought he really was going to throw up, he kneeled down and cradled the toilet bowl. But it passed and he resumed sitting on the closed seat, dousing himself with the water-cold rag until he felt steady enough to dress. He had no idea how long he sat. When he got back to the bedroom she was gone. He dressed slowly in sweats and tennis shoes and went downstairs. He still felt nauseous but not to the point of throwing up. It was her turn to be sitting in front of the fire staring. He went into the kitchen and began making himself a cup of coffee. She appeared. He looked at her. He couldn't read her: what would it be—frightened solicitude or irritable disgust or pieces of all of the above. He realized he didn't care right then.

"Why are you dressed?" she said flatly.

"Because I'm going to go get my boys."

"It's two A.M., David. Let's just undress and go to bed. We'll get them in the morning." It was a maternal voice, placating.

"No," he said.

"You can't just go barging over there and knock on the door," she said. She was angry now. "My mother will have a heart attack."

"Then call her and tell her I'm coming."

"David, be reasonable."

"If you don't call, I will knock on the door."

"You're not OK to drive."

"I am OK. Where are your keys? I need your car because you have the seat in it."

She got up and went to find her purse in the den. She came out, put it down, and rustled around to find the keys.

"Let me drive," she said.

"Give me the keys," he said.

She hesitated, then handed them to him. "Please be careful, David," she said.

"I always am," he said.

It was cold and clear like the previous night and the streets were almost completely deserted. David drove slowly, not so slowly he might attract a cop. You had to split the difference: not too fast, not too slow. Either was a giveaway. He felt reasonably sober, but still a little jazzed up from all of it: pills, booze, sex, if that's what you could call it.

Everything felt surreal and yet sharply etched at the same time. The houses under the street lamps. The big blue recycling bins. The leafless trees. As if they'd all been cut out with some big, sharp scissors and pasted against the night. On Wilshire, he passed the Christmas tree lots, not yet with trees, but full of big, bulbous pumpkins left from Halloween, hundreds of them, looking—David thought—lonesome and slightly ghoulish. They'd been given a Thanksgiving spin, big gaudy paper turkeys planted on top of some of them. It was imminent—Thanksgiving. Then Christmas. Time for more mitts. What had he done to his marriage? What had they done? He didn't want to think too hard about any of it right now. He just wanted to get from here to there, down this street, and up this side street to Aileen's condo. He had to see his boys because they always clarified his heart. He wanted to feel something real and sweet after what had happened.

When he pulled up, the light was on in Aileen's living-room window. Marcia had clearly called. He got out of the car, but just then her door opened and she came down the walk. She was holding Kyle, who was more or less still asleep—he made a groggy noise, David heard—while Trevor, his favorite stuffed bear in his arms, followed behind. David knelt down and picked him up.

"Daddy," Trevor said. "It's late."

"I know, sweetie, but we have to get up early if we want to get to Disneyland."

"Oh, Daddy," Trevor screeched.

"Shh, we don't want to wake everybody else up."

"What about Kyle? Don't you think we should tell him so he can sleep excited?"

David kissed his forehead as he strapped him in. Then he carefully took Kyle from Aileen's arms—both still doing the eye-avoiding game, for which he was grateful—and buckled him into the carseat.

"Thanks," he said to her. "We'll call you tomorrow. Today, I guess it is."

On the drive home, Trevor was excitedly talking about Disneyland—the rides he was going to take. None of that baby stuff like the teacups. You or Mommy will have to take Kyle. I can go on the bigger stuff. David kept trying to shh him, but only half-heartedly. His babble was a balm. Back they went by the pumpkins and the turkeys, which Trevor was too excited even to notice. David let his son's chatter wash over him, but he was not really hearing the words anymore. He knew that he had now caused damage to his marriage and would have to try to fix it. It was no longer just Marcia. With his stubborn sorrow (it really wasn't about pride; he wouldn't cop to that) he had bruised it, shamed it, helped make it tawdry—a dance of dildos and psychobabble. Had he no balls? Could he not have stopped it all and just pulled himself together? Could he not have just toughed it out and gotten on with it, stopped her from her effortfully vulgar and tender women's-mag stab at marital rehab. It was all so demeaning. And he'd been a willing participant—unmoored as he was by her defection. Now, he'd have to make it right. Or try to. Now she'd have to forgive him. And wouldn't that give our fair-haired Helen a good empathetic laugh? Welcome back, Mr. Sanderson. Welcome back, welcome back. He could hear them all now, the forgiveness groupies, craning in their seats to look at him with his lovely wife, Marcia. But that wasn't going to happen. That much he knew. No more groups, no more pills, no more shrinks. That was over. He would be quiet and try to put things back together. He was still a little blurry, more than—from the combination of booze and pills and his late recent techno-onanistic display—and he knew he'd have to wait 'til tomorrow or the next day or the next, when things really got out of his system, to assess adequately the damage. He hoped he hadn't hurt her too badly because he didn't want to lose her. He realized that that's what it had all been about: the terror of losing her. All he'd done, in his fear, was up the ante, push the envelope. But she wasn't going anywhere, was she? She did love him—still, didn't she? Look at the antic-romantic lengths she was willing to go for him. Well, she was sure as shit off her pedestal now. It made him sad.

He couldn't help it. OK, you weren't supposed to want them on the pedestal. That was macho, retro crap. All right, he was getting it. He might be a slow learner, but the message was coming through loud and clear. He'd been a fool, the last of the great romantics. Everybody was always blathering on about the uncommitted male. Well, he was the absurd opposite: the besottedly committed male. He would have to downshift his ardor. That had already happened, he realized, during their pill-and-porno-laden romp through marital reconstruction and that, too, made him sad. Their old bastard shrink would have the last laugh after all: they would now be one of those evolved couples, survivors. OK. He could live with that. Things had shifted. He had resisted mightily that shift and he now allowed himself a small nibble of pride over that fact—even though his resistance had been a little wobbly and a little whiny and—oh, shit, OK—a little unmanly. He hadn't exactly taken a colossal whack at resistance. He'd gone along with the program, more or less. Nobody dragged him to the good doctor or force-fed him drugs. Oh no, he'd played along while jousting with his "saviors," including his wife. Jab, jab. So much for resistance. But he'd take it right now, if only to bolster his soiled pride. All right, so it was about pride, too. He wanted her to want him forever and ever, only him—no sideways glances, certainly no adulterous automotive escapades—amen. But that hadn't happened. And he didn't know what lay ahead. All he knew at this moment was that he was, for better or worse, still a deeply married man on the way home with his boys (Wasn't that what he was doing out here in the wee small hours—bringing them back to her as a reminder, a gift, a peace offering—the best one he could possibly think of?) and on the way to one hell of a hangover.

He turned onto their street, Trevor never breaking verbal stride, and up into the driveway. He unstrapped Trevor, who bolted for the door, then gently lifted Kyle. He, too, was finally getting heavier. Marcia was there, door open, Trevor now yammering at her about Disneyland.

"Daddy promised, he promised."

"He did, did he?" she said, as David moved by her, without really looking at her, and up the stairs with Kyle in his arms. He was too exhausted to talk and, after all that had been done and ingested, he didn't trust himself anyway. Not yet. Kyle was in his pajamas with a parka over them. David laid him down and slipped off the jacket and his shoes, then covered him with the blanket and spread.

"Trevie," he called down, "come on up here."

Father and son met in the hall, then went hand in hand to Trevor's bedroom.

"Hop in," he said to Trevor, pulling back the bedcovers.

"Do you want to have a sleepover, Daddy, like before?" Trevor said.

"Not tonight, punkie. Daddy's going to his own bed. Big doings tomorrow."

He turned off the light and shut the door. He stood in the darkened hall. The boys were home now, tucked in. He listened: he had no idea where Marcia was. Maybe it was her turn to sleep somewhere else, in some other room. He was tempted to go find her, lie down beside her, but thought better of it. A wave of nausea came up from his belly but he swallowed it down. He realized how exhausted he was. Maybe he would be able to sleep after all, even without the pills and double Scotches. He wasn't sure. It had been a long time since he'd slept without taking something. Their bedroom was dark. He lay down on top of the cover. He felt sorry about all of it. But it was over. He hoped they would stay married. He expected they would stay married. But nothing anymore was certain. The only thing he knew for certain was that tomorrow he, David Sanderson, was taking his two little boys to Disneyland.

ACKNOWLEDGMENTS

———ᴧᴧᴧ———

I would like to thank:

My longtime agent, Lynn Nesbit, for her superb guidance and early enthusiasm for this book.

My editor, Leigh Haber, for her out-of-the-blocks excitement over the manuscript and for her sharp eye and delicate hand. Also, all her colleagues at Hyperion—notably, publisher Ellen Archer—for sharing that excitement.

Judy Kessler, my lifetime friend, exhorter and trusted early reader.

My husband, Karl Fleming, who reads my work with respect and pride and an editor's attentiveness and makes my life possible.

And finally, the writers, past and present, whose words have made the world seem bearable and beautiful.